the twilight saga

THE COMPLETE FILM ARCHIVE

Memories, Mementos, and Other Treasures
From the Creative Team Behind the Beloved Motion Pictures

BY ROBERT ABELE

AN INSIGHT EDITIONS BOOK

LITTLE, BROWN AND COMPANY

CONTENTS

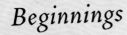

Beginnings

Complications

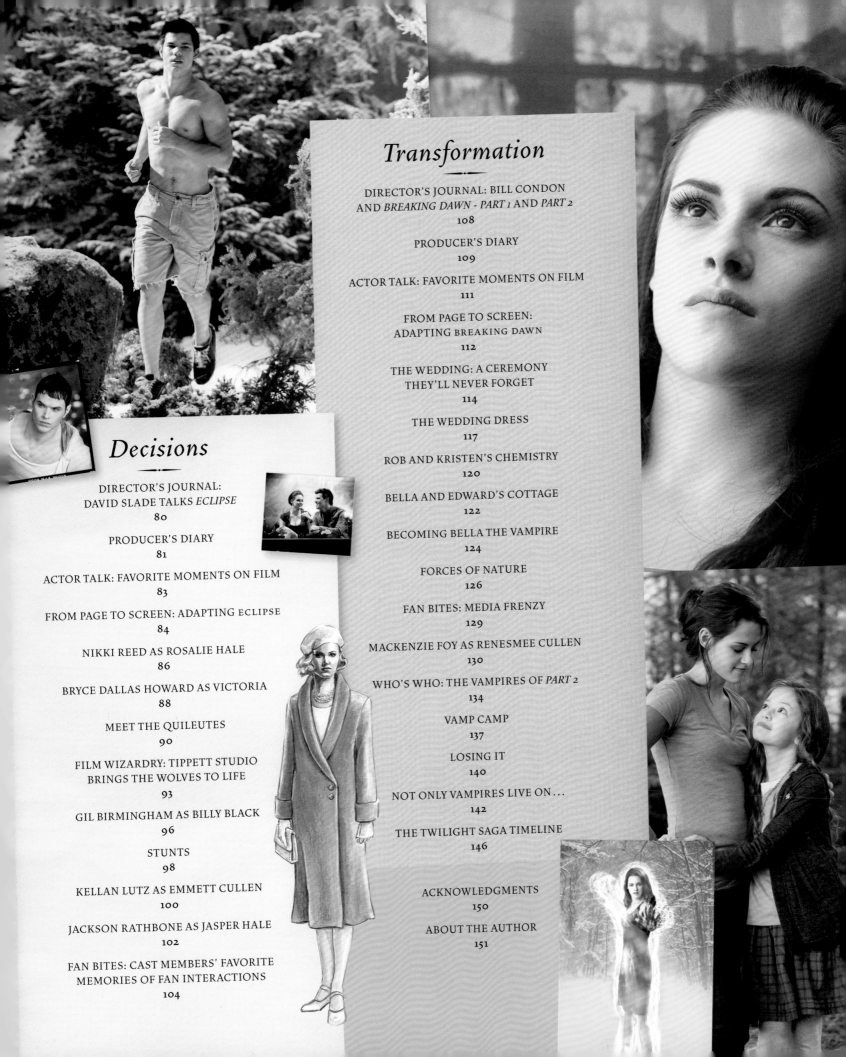

Transformation

Decisions

Bella and Edward began in a dream. The dream became words and so entered the hearts of millions. The words became moving pictures and so reached millions more. And now, here, for the first time is the complete film archive, from inception to conclusion, as told by the people who honored that dream, nurtured those words, and crafted the pictures, bringing Bella and Edward's story to life and beyond . . .

THE START
OF A SAGA

> ❝It was very clear. I was an observer. When I woke up, I sat there with my eyes closed, thinking about it . . . It was like reading a great book when you don't want to put it down; you want to know what happens next. So, I just laid there imagining.❞ —STEPHENIE MEYER

I t's hard to know what goes through an author's mind when a dream blossoms into a book and then transforms again onto a flickering movie screen. But like the lesson Bella Swan learned on her journey, one thing was for sure: finding the right partner was key.

Summit Entertainment's president of production Erik Feig made it clear they wanted to capture on-screen the same tone and spirit that millions of readers loved on the page. Screenwriter Melissa Rosenberg worked tirelessly to ensure that TWILIGHT fans got an experience that honored the novels, yet delivered the kind of visual, concentrated thrill that only comes from movies. It would be a celebration of Stephenie Meyer's creation—different but still a blood relative.

And the rest is history. The release of the *Twilight* film brought even more readers to Stephenie's novels. With the publication of BREAKING DAWN, the book series was drawing to a close just as the *The Twilight Saga* motion pictures were sparking an interest in Bella's world all over again. Stephenie's dream would now be cemented as a worldwide cultural phenomenon. ■

FROM LEFT: Justin Chon, Michael Welch, Stephenie Meyer, Christian Serratos, Anna Kendrick, Gregory Tyree Boyce, and *Twilight* director Catherine Hardwicke

Production Office
Twilight Prods, LLC

twilight

Director: Catherine Hardwicke
Producers: Wyck Godfrey,
Mark Morgan, Greg Mooradian.
Exec. Prod: Karen Rosenfelt, Guy Oseary
Michele Imperato Stabile.
Co-Producer: Jamie Marshall
Writer: Melissa Rosenberg

**CREW CALL:
7AM ON LOCATION**
(Approx. Travel Time= 48 MINUTES)
(Check Back for PRE-CALLS)
REHEARSAL: TBD
SHOOTING CALL: TBD

CURRENT SCRIPT: CHERRY 3/31/08   **PLE.

SET	SCENE	CAST	D-N	P
COMPANY REPORT TO CREW PARKING. SHUTTLE TO BASE CAMP. S				
EXT: CULLEN HOUSE-TREE TO TREE-PLATFORM #3	88pt. (C)	1, 2, 1X, 2X	D17	
Edward holds onto Bella. He shows off the view. SB #11.		(BG x 0)		
EXT: CULLEN HOUSE-TREE TO TREE-PLATFORM #2	88pt. (C)	1, 2, 1X, 2X	D17	
Edward holds onto Bella. He asks her to trust him. SB #7.		(BG x 0)		
TBD B CAMERA WHEN TIME PERMITS:	95pt.	—	D19	
EXT: FIELD	95pt.	2	D19	
Leaves blowing in the field (baseball field).				
Edward running.				

CREW: RUGGED LOCATION. PLEASE DRESS ACCORDINGLY.   THANK YOU.

#	CAST	STATUS	CHARACTER	PICK-UP	MAKE-UP
1	Kristen Stewart (K)	W	Bella Swan	6:12AM	7AM
2	Rob Pattinson	W	Edward Cullen	5:42AM	6:30AM
3	Billy Burke	H	Charlie Swan		*HOLD*
4	Ashley Greene	H	Alice Cullen		*HOLD*
5	Nikki Reed	H	Rosalie Cullen		*HOLD*
6	Jackson Rathbone	H	Jasper Cullen		*HOLD*
7	Kellan Lutz	H	Emmett Cullen		*HOLD*
8	Peter Facinelli	H	Dr. Cullen		*HOLD*
10	Taylor Lautner	TR	Jacob Black		**TRAVEL TO
11	Anna Kendrick	H	Jessica		*HOLD*
12	Michael Welch	H	Mike Newton		*HOLD*
13	Justin Chon	TR	Eric		**TRAVEL TO
14	Christian Serratos (K)	FIT	Angela	9:12AM	10AM FIT
15	Gil Birmingham	H	Billy Black		*HOLD*
20	Gregory Tyree Boyce	TR	Tyler		**TRAVEL TO
23	Jose Zuniga	WF	Mr. Molina	WILL NOTIFY IF N	
PD	Katie Powers	WF	Bella Photo Double	5:42AM	--
XX	Xuyen "Sammy" Valdivia	WF	Assist. Stunt Coord.	5:12AM	6AM
1X	Helena Barrett	WF	Bella Stunt Double	5:12AM	6AM
2X	Paul Darnell	WF	Edward Stunt Double	5:48AM	--
X	Bob McDougall	WF	Utility Stunt Rigger	5:48AM	--
X	Matt Davis	WF	Utility Stunt Rigger		

**NO VISITORS ALLOWED ON SET WITHOUT PRIOR APPROVAL FROM
***No Forced Calls Without Prior Approval From the UPM or Prod. Supervisor. All Calls Subject To

STAND-INS/ATMOSPHERE			SPECIAL INSTR
STAND-INS:	Art:		Platforms.
	Sp. Equip:		1 x 30' Techno, 1 x E
	Greens:		2 x staked trees
	VFX:		Wire removal.
ATMOSPHERE:	Costumes:		Shoes w/ spikes or
	Stills/Props:		Shoot stills with Ch
	Stunts:		Safety harnesses, s
	Publicity:		
	Props:		Stills-fishing gack,

CAST PICKUPS TO SET
PU #1   PU from residence
PU #2   PU from B @ 6:12
PU #3   PU from M @ 9:12

CREW / STUNTS PICKUPS
PU #1   PU from Lloyd @
        Jeannie Van Phue
PU #2   PU from Marriott
PU #3   PU from Lloyd @
PU #4   BRKF VAN PU from Lloyd @
PU #5   PU from residen

> " You always had to wear your ID badge, or you were threatened to be fired. And I'm the worst person in the world, because not only do I not like to wear badges, but I also can quite easily forget them. So I would sleep with mine. I would take showers with it every day. Sometimes when it was cold, I'd be like, 'What is that?' And it would be my wet badge. So I held on to that badge. I was too horrified, with all the security. Even now, I don't like to talk about it. "
>
> —JEAN BLACK (MAKEUP DESIGNER, *BREAKING DAWN*)

THE TWILIGHT SAGA SET CONTAINMENT
STANDARDS AND PRACTICES

SECURITY LAYER ONE: PERSONAL BODYGUARDS
A bodyguard each for Kristen Stewart, Robert Pattinson, and Taylor Lautner. "If things got really crazy," says Bill, "we might assign them two."

SECURITY LAYER TWO: UNIFORMED OFFICERS
Trained individuals—primarily career SWAT police officers—to enforce trespassing laws. "When they caught paparazzi sneaking through the woods, or fans doing things they shouldn't, they'd make them aware of the fact that they were in violation."

SECURITY LAYER THREE: DEPUTIZED CREW MEMBERS
Production-staff security hired to monitor activity of all electronics—not to mention people—on set. Says Bill, "They would watch the crew full-time."

BADGES
The de rigueur accessory for every last person on set, color-coded by department: crew, marketing, equipment deliveries, etc. And if someone lost or forgot a badge? "They weren't allowed on set until it was rectified," says Bill. "The crew very quickly got the idea that we were serious about this."

ZERO-VISITORS POLICY
"Carried forward right from the get-go when I was on *New Moon*," Bill says.

"SET BLACKS"
More than two dozen twenty-by-ten-foot frames, covered in black fabric and propped up to shield filming. According to Bill, grips were employed specifically "to build, maintain, and shift these black screens from location to location, shot to shot." Look toward the set and that's all you'd see.

UMBRELLAS
For zone coverage of a costumed actor, nothing beats a classic. "When it came to paparazzi on a long lens in the bushes or on a mountainside trying to get a picture of Kristen or Rob or Taylor doing an intimate rehearsal," explains Bill, "layer-one security always carried umbrellas."

NO ELECTRONICS
Recording-device-free stock phones were provided, but outside phones and cameras were strictly forbidden.

Beginnings

Catherine Hardwicke imitating Victoria in the production office

DIRECTOR'S JOURNAL

CATHERINE HARDWICKE AND THE BIRTH OF THE *TWILIGHT* FILMS

When Catherine Hardwicke was first approached with the concept of turning TWILIGHT into a film, it was the promise of the images that the novel opened in her head that sold it for her. "I thought, I've seen vampires in dingy, dark streets in London in the middle of the night, but I'd never seen beautiful pale vampires in mossy woods," Catherine recalls. "Plus, I love the Pacific Northwest, with the trees, the mist, the green of it all, and I wanted to see that. I thought it could be striking."

Indeed, over the forty-two days that Catherine was filming *Twilight* in cold, rainy Portland, Oregon, in the spring of 2008, a number of memorable visuals were captured, which relayed the beginning of Bella Swan and Edward Cullen's romance: ethereal forests through which a pocket of light made an already exquisite-looking vampire sparkle further; a date atop towering trees; a gravity-defying baseball game; a deadly showdown in a mirror-bedecked ballet studio; and a twinkly lit prom dance between young lovers who, at the very beginning of their romantic journey, had already been through more than most couples endure in a lifetime. ➤

(ABOVE) An early sketch of Catherine's depicting an underwater kiss

(RIGHT) Catherine directs Kristen and Rob in the meadow.

➤ When it came to more intimate moments between Kristen Stewart and Robert Pattinson, Catherine's protectiveness for the acting process was in full force. "We try to create the right environment so they feel comfortable being that way," she says. "One of the things is not to have lookie-loos on the set, but try to be respectful and create a space. If it's a bedroom scene, just try to have them, the cinematographer, and the sound guy. And not have people talking, joking, running around."

Catherine and *Twilight*'s director of photography, Elliot Davis, worked to maintain that closeness between the actors on-screen and to anchor the story from Bella's perspective. "Most of the scenes, it's how Bella's experiencing the world," says Catherine. "And I think Elliot's a master with moving and reacting to actors' feelings and emotions in a very organic way. He also lights sets beautifully, not too sappy but with a nice edge. He almost breathes with the actors. He's another actor, really. He flows with the feeling of the piece, and those are the parts that are most alive."

Because Stephenie Meyer's original portrayal of the vampires had them seeking to blend in with society—at a hospital or in a high school lunchroom—Catherine looked for a color scheme that wasn't too ostentatious. "The whole movie had a controlled palette," she says. "Blues, blue-grays, silvers, whites, blacks . . . those are the only colors the Cullens could have, to make them nice-looking kids but also, in a way, different. You don't see flashes of orange and yellow."

While the movie's hues were set in stone, what the actors were enlisted to do on camera was often fluid. Improvisation was encouraged, ideas for scenes and moments were tossed around, and some were even filmed. Michael Welch, who played the character Mike Newton, recalls, "There was a moment when we were on the field trip, when Catherine had me pop my head in from between some plants and go 'Hell-OOOOO!' in a high-pitched voice, and then pop back in again. I mean, the shot was specifically set up for that. It didn't make it in, but it was pretty silly. The thing was, she wanted us to be a realistic small-town group of high school kids. That's not a particularly structured thing, so we didn't go about it in a particularly structured way." ➤

BELLA – COLOR PALETTE

COLORS OF ARCTIC WOLF

CULLENS COLOR PALETTE

❝ We were at the high school, and we couldn't shoot because it was too sunny. So Catherine went over to a bunch of extras and was like, 'Come on, let's pull the clouds in!' So we all began pretending to throw ropes into the sky and pulling. And suddenly clouds were coming in, and then we got our shot! I just loved how she was on top of it, and very much the catalyst for making everything work. With Catherine's energy, everything felt like art. ❞ —KELLAN LUTZ (EMMETT)

Producer Wyck Godfrey describes Catherine's demonstrative energy as "ragged, raw [and] exciting" on set. "And as a result, it's able to transfer to the performances," he notes. "There's a rawness and immediacy that isn't overly rehearsed or practiced, which makes it feel more real."

It's all about making a film that doesn't feel like a book on tape, explains the director. "A lot of the book is internal, and I wanted to make it more visual and cinematic, so that it would be like giving a bonus to fans. Where two people are sitting in a car talking, I'm going to put them in the woods, running, experiencing the nature that they're connected to. That whole treetop sequence, that's not in the book, but the spirit of it, I would say, is in the book because I wanted a scene that was like, 'Wow, what does it feel like when you're dizzy, madly in love, and anything's possible?'"

Nowadays, when Catherine has a chance to look at her movie, it's usually in the context of showing a scene to students in high schools or colleges. It always serves to remind her of how much she enjoyed putting Stephenie's love story on the screen. "I get to see people reliving and loving those scenes again," she says. "I love it. I had a great time working on that movie. You know, as a director you obsess over details; you try to get everything right. Usually you do that, and people might love the feeling of the movie, but not notice the details or be able to quote every line. Well, on *Twilight*, people did! It's great to have people appreciate that level of detail." ∎

⚬ PRODUCER'S DIARY ⚬

Jamie Marshall (assistant director), Michelle Imperato Stabile (line producer), Wyck Godfrey, and Catherine Hardwicke

Producer Wyck Godfrey, who'd worked with Catherine Hardwicke previously, sees Twilight as showcasing the director's unique sympathy for the intensity of first love. "It feels like life and death, like the world will end if things don't work out," says Wyck. "Catherine manages to capture the internal turmoil of a teenager on-screen better than any other director. With Bella and Edward, the whole world fell away when they experienced their connection, and that's all about the way she shoots her characters. Very handheld, close to the faces, everything in looks and touches, very sensual."

According to Wyck, Catherine was the epitome of a filmmaker who had a clear vision in her head of what needed to be on-screen. "And like many great artists, she's single minded in her effort to get it, so a lot of times, getting all the pieces of the puzzle is difficult because it's specific to her mind. A painter can just go paint it, but a director's got to galvanize a group of people and communicate to all of them. So there's a ragged, raw, exciting energy on set with Catherine, because she's very emotional and demonstrative in the way she communicates that vision to everybody."

Ned Bellamy (Waylon Forge) and Catherine Hardwicke in the diner

Catherine Hardwicke directs Kristen Stewart in the lab scene.

ACTOR TALK

FAVORITE MOMENTS ON FILM

"There are so many [scenes] that I love, but one of them that I really like is in the first movie, where Edward saves Bella from getting crushed by the vehicle, and he stops it with his hand. Then they're staring at each other, and it's silence. That's a really cool moment. I love that scene. It was just really intense." —Jodelle Ferland (Bree)

"I love that scene in *Twilight* where Bella and Edward first have to sit next to each other in their chemistry class, and I feel like that moment, to me, is when the popularity of the franchise was sealed. They have so much chemistry!" —Julia Jones (Leah)

"I have to say, the baseball scene in *Twilight* is pretty cool, with the special effects, and Catherine Hardwicke has such an eye for style. The way adrenaline and thrill all come together—I thought that's what was cool about that." —Sarah Clarke (Renée)

"One of the most memorable scenes for me will always be from the first film, when Robert picks Kristen up, and they go running as fast as they can through the trees. And he's just going at lightning pace. He puts her on piggyback and says, 'Hang on.' Really romantic. And as an audience member, it's such a girlie thing to enjoy, that you're just going for this ride, but that's really memorable to me." —Toni Trucks (Mary)

FROM PAGE TO SCREEN
ADAPTING TWILIGHT

For a novel to work on-screen, changes invariably have to be made. The saga's talented screenwriter, Melissa Rosenberg, explains, "[Catherine Hardwicke and I] really consciously made Bella more proactive, which is essential to movie storytelling. In a book, you're inside their mind; you can get what their thought process is. But you can't do that in a movie. You have to move things forward."

Typically that means cutting down conversations, turning internalized thoughts into action, and looking for new ways to reveal information. Melissa cites as an example the way she changed Bella's discovery of her mystifying, enchanting, gorgeous classmate's *true* nature. "In the book, it's rolled out in a relaxed way; it's not an explosive moment. In the film, it made more sense for it to be a *moment*."

Whereas in the book it's Jacob Black's beach chat with Bella that plants the word *vampire* in her brain, the movie initiates a multistep process that allows her to put two and two together herself. "Bella does question him in the book, but it's a gentler series of conversations," says Melissa. "In the movie, it's condensed. She has an idea what he is, walks past him in a nonverbal invitation to follow her into the woods, and in that moment confronts him. That's a proactive approach to the character: She's actively pursuing the information. It marks a clear mid-point, where everything changes. 'You're a vampire, I accept you, we're together.'"

At this point in a screenplay, another conflict rises to the surface. Rather than leave the introduction of not-so-charitable vampires James, Victoria, and Laurent for the story's last quarter, Melissa chose to bring them forward as a threat from the beginning of the movie. ▶

TWILIGHT

by
Melissa Rosenberg

Based on the Novel By
Stephenie Meyer

10/31/07 - White Shooting Draft
2/13/08 - Blue Shooting Draft
2/25/08 - Pink Revisions
3/3/08 - Yellow Revisions
3/10/08 - Green Revisions
3/13/08 - Goldenrod Revisions
3/14/08 - Buff Revisions
3/18/08 - Salmon Revisions
3/31/08 - Cherry Revisions
4/4/08 - Tan Revisions

© 2007
Summit Entertainment, LLC
All Rights Reserved

...board art maps out ...for the run through ...rees in *Twilight*.

Rob getting prepped for visual-effects shooting to get that "sparkle"

> "It serves a couple of purposes," she says. "One, it layers in something that is ultimately going to be our final battle. But it also really distinguishes the difference between the Cullen clan and the rest of the vampire community. The Cullens are weirdos in the world of vampires. And since you see James kill someone before Edward is fully exposed as a vampire, you don't know whether Edward is going to go that way or not. It also gets Charlie Swan involved in the story, because he's the one investigating these events, and it's his friend—an invention of mine—who's killed."

Another change Melissa made was moving the introduction of Jacob up to Bella's first arrival in Forks, rather than on the beach at La Push. "I just wanted to begin to establish the reservation. But when I was doing that, I didn't know about NEW MOON. I hadn't read it. Of course, the producers had read all the books. One of them said, 'You know, Jacob plays heavily in the future.' I didn't even know."

Melissa says she deliberately didn't read NEW MOON and ECLIPSE when she wrote the screenplay for *Twilight* because it was important for her to approach it the way an audience member unfamiliar with the series would: with fresh eyes, open to a new story. "I wanted to make sure I was establishing the world, so that it stands alone, so that it's not reliant on mythology that's to come in the future." ▪

WELCOME TO FORKS

Thanks to Stephenie Meyer, the sign in the state of Washington that reads "The City of Forks Welcomes You"—with its green, planked wood and raised white lettering—may be the most famous town-identifying symbol in pop culture today. That's because Forks is where she sends heroine Bella Swan on the first page of TWILIGHT. This small logging community and scenic river region has been a prime destination for fans of her beloved tale of rain forest–dwelling vampires, proud shape-shifters, and eternally young love.

When the books were turned into the megapopular movie series, however, Forks multiplied in a sense. That authentic welcome sign may zip past Bella as she rides into town with her father at the start of Catherine Hardwicke's film *Twilight*, but what you see in that first movie is a city taking on a role, not unlike an actor. The demands of moviemaking meant Portland, Oregon, was called on to play Forks, as well as surrounding locales St. Helens and Vernonia. Then, as subsequent movies decamped to British Columbia, the Vancouver area became Forks. ➤

Signpost outside the Forks Timber Museum

Mounted deer head in Forks

THE MANY FACES OF FORKS

FORKS, WASHINGTON

AREA: 3.1 square miles

POPULATION: Approx. 3,600

SURROUNDINGS: Olympic National Park

ATTRACTIONS: Salmon and steelhead fishing

INDUSTRIES: Agriculture and forestry

RAINFALL: 211 days per year

PRE-*TWILIGHT*: 10,000 visitors per year

POST-*TWILIGHT*: 73,000 visitors per year and counting . . .

PORTLAND, OREGON (*TWILIGHT*)

AREA: 145.4 square miles

POPULATION: Approx. 600,000

SURROUNDINGS: Willamette River

ST. HELENS, OREGON (*TWILIGHT*)

AREA: 5.3 square miles

POPULATION: Approx. 12,600

SURROUNDINGS: Columbia River

VERNONIA, OREGON (*TWILIGHT*)

AREA: 1.6 square miles

POPULATION: Approx. 2,500

SURROUNDINGS: Nehalem River, Oregon Coast

VANCOUVER, BRITISH COLUMBIA (*NEW MOON, ECLIPSE, BREAKING DAWN - PART 1 AND PART 2*)

AREA: 44.39 square miles

POPULATION: Approx. 603,000

SURROUNDINGS: Burrard Peninsula, Stanley Park

SQUAMISH, BRITISH COLUMBIA (*BREAKING DAWN - PART 1 AND PART 2*)

AREA: 40.49 square miles

POPULATION: Approx. 17,500

SURROUNDINGS: Stawamus Chief, Coast Mountains

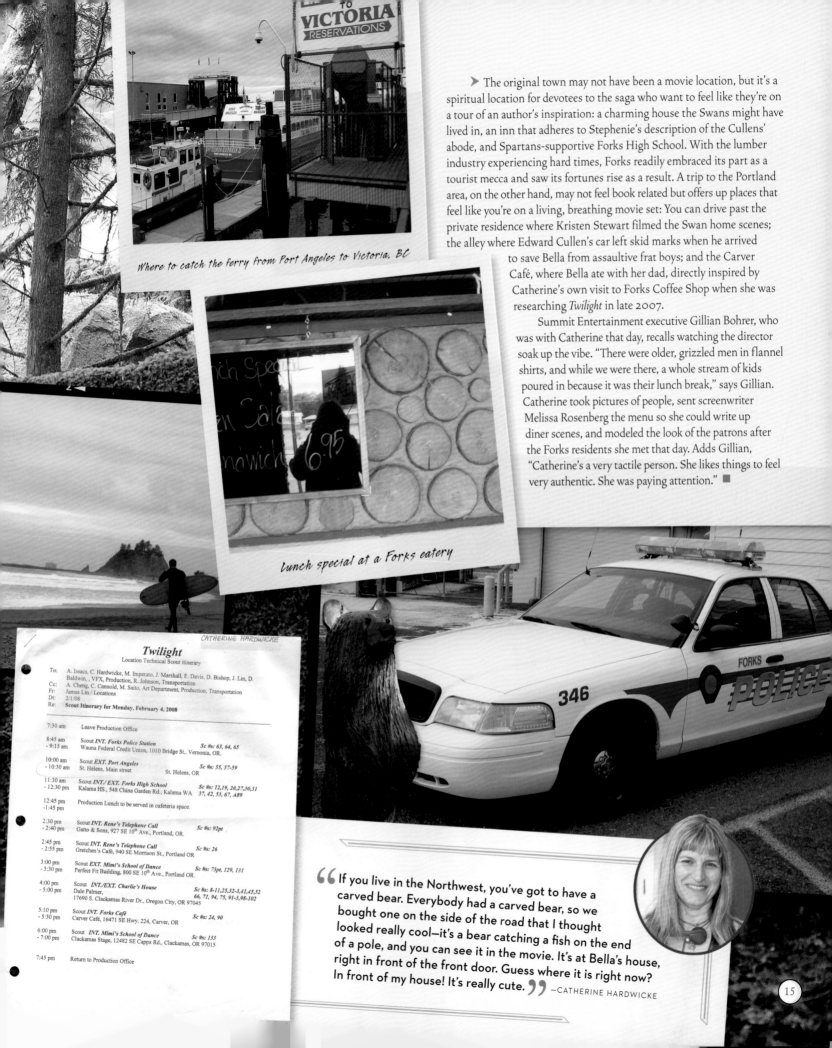

Where to catch the ferry from Port Angeles to Victoria, BC

Lunch special at a Forks eatery

➤ The original town may not have been a movie location, but it's a spiritual location for devotees to the saga who want to feel like they're on a tour of an author's inspiration: a charming house the Swans might have lived in, an inn that adheres to Stephenie's description of the Cullens' abode, and Spartans-supportive Forks High School. With the lumber industry experiencing hard times, Forks readily embraced its part as a tourist mecca and saw its fortunes rise as a result. A trip to the Portland area, on the other hand, may not feel book related but offers up places that feel like you're on a living, breathing movie set: You can drive past the private residence where Kristen Stewart filmed the Swan home scenes; the alley where Edward Cullen's car left skid marks when he arrived to save Bella from assaultive frat boys; and the Carver Café, where Bella ate with her dad, directly inspired by Catherine's own visit to Forks Coffee Shop when she was researching *Twilight* in late 2007.

Summit Entertainment executive Gillian Bohrer, who was with Catherine that day, recalls watching the director soak up the vibe. "There were older, grizzled men in flannel shirts, and while we were there, a whole stream of kids poured in because it was their lunch break," says Gillian. Catherine took pictures of people, sent screenwriter Melissa Rosenberg the menu so she could write up diner scenes, and modeled the look of the patrons after the Forks residents she met that day. Adds Gillian, "Catherine's a very tactile person. She likes things to feel very authentic. She was paying attention." ■

CATHERINE HARDWICKE

Twilight
Location Technical Scout itinerary

To: A. Issacs, C. Hardwicke, M. Imperato, J. Marshall, E. Davis, D. Bishop, J. Lin, D. Baldwin, , VFX, Production, R. Johnson, Transportation
Cc: A. Cheng, C. Cannold, M. Saito, Art Department, Production, Transportation
Fr: James Lin / Locations
Dt: 2/1/08
Re: **Scout Itinerary for Monday, February 4, 2008**

7:30 am	Leave Production Office	
8:45 am - 9:15 am	Scout *INT. Forks Police Station* Wauna Federal Credit Union, 1010 Bridge St., Vernonia, OR.	Sc #s: 63, 64, 65
10:00 am - 10:30 am	Scout *EXT. Port Angeles* St. Helens, Main street St. Helens, OR	Sc #s: 55, 57-59
11:30 am - 12:30 pm	Scout *INT./EXT. Forks High School* Kalama HS., 548 China Garden Rd., Kalama WA	Sc #s: 12,19, 20,27,30,31 37, 42, 53, 67, A89
12:45 pm -1:45 pm	Production Lunch to be served in cafeteria space.	
2:30 pm - 2:40 pm	Scout *INT. Rene's Telephone Call* Gatto & Sons, 927 SE 10th Ave., Portland, OR.	Sc #s: 92pt
2:45 pm - 2:55 pm	Scout *INT. Rene's Telephone Call* Gretchen's Café, 940 SE Morrison St., Portland OR	Sc #s: 26
3:00 pm - 3:30 pm	Scout *EXT. Mimi's School of Dance* Perfect Fit Building, 800 SE 10th Ave., Portland OR.	Sc #s: 73pt, 129, 131
4:00 pm - 5:00 pm	Scout *INT./EXT. Charlie's House* Dale Palmer, 17690 S. Clackamas River Dr., Oregon City, OR 97045	Sc #s: 8-11,25,32-3,41,45,52 66, 71, 94, 75, 91-3,98-102
5:10 pm - 5:30 pm	Scout *INT. Forks Café* Carver Café, 16471 SE Hwy. 224, Carver, OR	Sc #s: 24, 90
6:00 pm - 7:00 pm	Scout *INT. Mimi's School of Dance* Clackamas Stage, 12482 SE Capps Rd., Clackamas, OR, 97015	Sc #s: 133
7:45 pm	Return to Production Office	

❝ If you live in the Northwest, you've got to have a carved bear. Everybody had a carved bear, so we bought one on the side of the road that I thought looked really cool—it's a bear catching a fish on the end of a pole, and you can see it in the movie. It's at Bella's house, right in front of the front door. Guess where it is right now? In front of my house! It's really cute. ❞ —CATHERINE HARDWICKE

Kristen Stewart as BELLA SWAN

When Kristen Stewart thinks about playing Bella Swan over the course of four years and five movies, she realizes just how comfortable it's been to take on the emotions, thoughts, and actions of Stephenie Meyer's committed, love-struck heroine. But it was a comfort born of zeal for who Bella was and what she fought for.

"I haven't had much experience playing characters I didn't love personally, where I would defend them, but in this case, it's been tenfold," says Kristen. "More so than anything in normal circumstances. Because if you're reading the books, and not studying them or appreciating them on some weird level, but if you're reading and experiencing them the way most of us who love it have, then you are her. So with Bella, I always completely inserted myself into the whole process, because I felt like that when I read it. It was like breathing." ➤

🎞 PRODUCER'S TAKE

"She had the hardest of jobs. Kristen is on-screen almost every moment, and she was often working when others weren't working. If they had days off, she usually didn't. But one of my earliest memories of Kristen is one of the fondest. It was one of the first days of shooting on *Twilight*, and it was the final battle in the ballet studio. Now, that's an incredibly raw, difficult scene for any seventeen-year-old actress, especially one who hasn't met anybody on set, to immediately be thrown across the floor and have to writhe in pain from being bitten. But I can remember, from the very moment she came on set, she was, 'All right, let's do it!' She'd slide herself across the floor, then say 'No, that wasn't good enough!' It's so much of a fantasy moment, to convey what it feels like to have venom coursing through your veins, to feel like you're burning up inside and dying. A lesser-committed actress might have just 'oohed' and 'aahed' her way through it, but Kristen embodied it in a way that made us all feel the intensity of it. It was so impressive, how she was so into getting it right, that we all thought, 'Thank God, we've got our Bella.' She was immediately great." —Wyck Godfrey

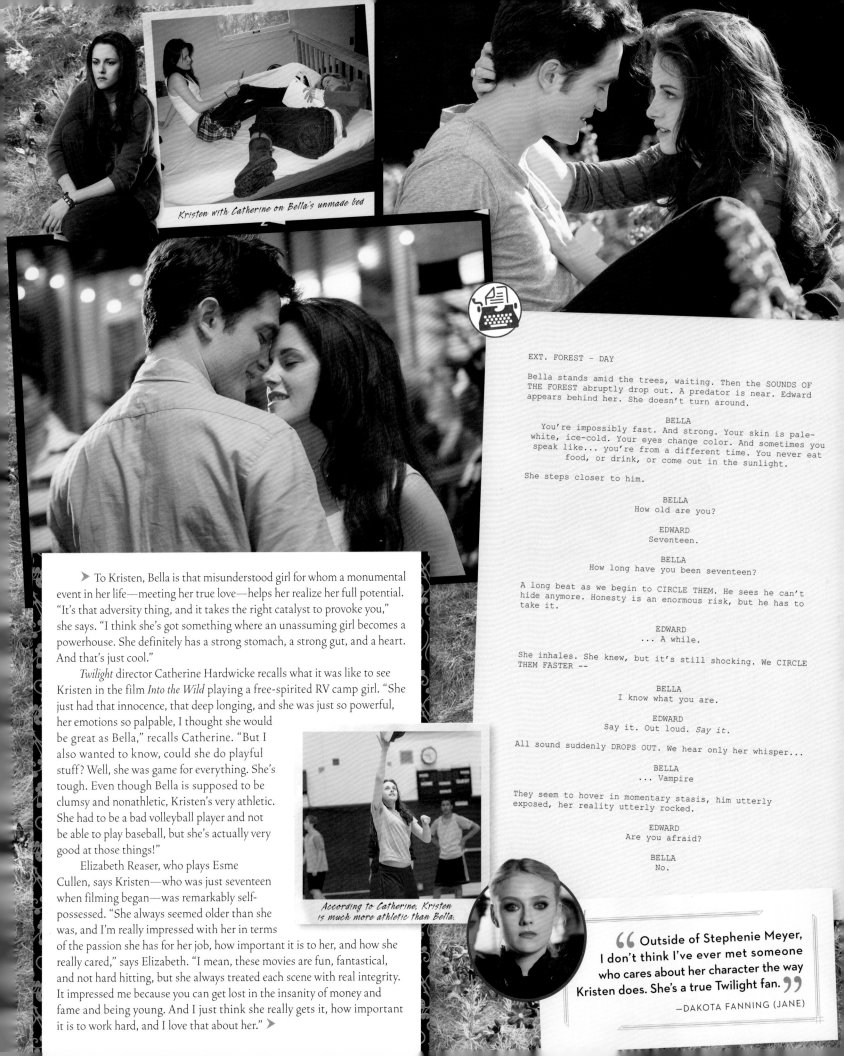

Kristen with Catherine on Bella's unmade bed

According to Catherine, Kristen is much more athletic than Bella.

To Kristen, Bella is that misunderstood girl for whom a monumental event in her life—meeting her true love—helps her realize her full potential. "It's that adversity thing, and it takes the right catalyst to provoke you," she says. "I think she's got something where an unassuming girl becomes a powerhouse. She definitely has a strong stomach, a strong gut, and a heart. And that's just cool."

Twilight director Catherine Hardwicke recalls what it was like to see Kristen in the film *Into the Wild* playing a free-spirited RV camp girl. "She just had that innocence, that deep longing, and she was just so powerful, her emotions so palpable, I thought she would be great as Bella," recalls Catherine. "But I also wanted to know, could she do playful stuff? Well, she was game for everything. She's tough. Even though Bella is supposed to be clumsy and nonathletic, Kristen's very athletic. She had to be a bad volleyball player and not be able to play baseball, but she's actually very good at those things!"

Elizabeth Reaser, who plays Esme Cullen, says Kristen—who was just seventeen when filming began—was remarkably self-possessed. "She always seemed older than she was, and I'm really impressed with her in terms of the passion she has for her job, how important it is to her, and how she really cared," says Elizabeth. "I mean, these movies are fun, fantastical, and not hard hitting, but she always treated each scene with real integrity. It impressed me because you can get lost in the insanity of money and fame and being young. And I just think she really gets it, how important it is to work hard, and I love that about her."

```
EXT. FOREST - DAY

Bella stands amid the trees, waiting. Then the SOUNDS OF
THE FOREST abruptly drop out. A predator is near. Edward
appears behind her. She doesn't turn around.

                         BELLA
        You're impossibly fast. And strong. Your skin is pale-
        white, ice-cold. Your eyes change color. And sometimes you
        speak like... you're from a different time. You never eat
           food, or drink, or come out in the sunlight.

She steps closer to him.

                         BELLA
                    How old are you?

                        EDWARD
                      Seventeen.

                         BELLA
               How long have you been seventeen?

A long beat as we begin to CIRCLE THEM. He sees he can't
hide anymore. Honesty is an enormous risk, but he has to
take it.

                        EDWARD
                      ... A while.

She inhales. She knew, but it's still shocking. We CIRCLE
THEM FASTER --

                         BELLA
                  I know what you are.

                        EDWARD
                Say it. Out loud. Say it.

All sound suddenly DROPS OUT. We hear only her whisper...

                         BELLA
                      ... Vampire

They seem to hover in momentary stasis, him utterly
exposed, her reality utterly rocked.

                        EDWARD
                   Are you afraid?

                         BELLA
                         No.
```

> **"** Outside of Stephenie Meyer, I don't think I've ever met someone who cares about her character the way Kristen does. She's a true Twilight fan. **"**
>
> —DAKOTA FANNING (JANE)

Kristen admits that sometimes she gets too wrapped up in preparing to shoot an emotional scene, like the breakup in *The Twilight Saga: New Moon*. A "shaky wave" is how she describes what she's riding in those moments. "It's not the greatest thing for me, but I need that. I need to be terrified, to feel that I could either bring life to it or ruin it. It's why I want to do this stuff."

Elsewhere, Kristen's intensity has led to some funnier interactions, like the time she approached Stephenie about playing Bella as a vampire the way the author imagined it. Kristen recounts, "I ran up and was like, 'How the [bleep] do I sound like wind chimes, Stephenie?!?' She was like 'What?' And I said, 'Don't you remember that you wrote that?' She said, 'Oh, don't worry, no one could ever sound like that.' And I said, 'I know, I'm just nervous. I'm sorry, I'll go.'" Kristen laughs at the memory. "I don't think she always understood when I was joking, but I loved talking to her about stuff. Her presence was so motivating."

By the time of *The Twilight Saga: Breaking Dawn*, Kristen was able to enjoy some of the peace that comes from knowing a character so well. "I knew fate wouldn't let certain parts of that movie be anything other than what we've all been waiting to do," she says. "Like the wedding. I loved that scene. I loved doing it. I knew something was happening that I would never forget. Though I had no idea what I was going to do when I walked down that aisle, I didn't care. I just felt completely how she felt."

That said, few aspects of the moviemaking process escaped her, as Bill Condon will attest. When Kristen saw a take of herself during the wedding sequence, she told the director, "It looks a little like I'm getting nauseous, and I think it's because the camera's a little high." Recalls Bill, "I was like 'Whoa.' She was right, and it made me a little embarrassed! I mean, she's been on so many sets, she's just a gifted, natural storyteller, and has a sense of how to do it visually."

(TOP) Kristen, Stephenie, and Taylor on the set of the *New Moon* movie-theater scene. (MIDDLE LEFT) Rehearsing the pregnancy scene. (MIDDLE RIGHT) Kristen and Rob in a *Breaking Dawn - Part 2* scene with Casey LaBow as Kate.

She's held on to a few mementos from the movies, including the first "weird, funky eco shoes" Bella wore from her "dork" days on *Twilight*, and the mood ring Bella's mom gives her. "It's interesting that I have that one instead of the wedding ring, but you know, OG. Original gangsta!"

Looking back on it all, Kristen feels especially grateful to have been a part of something that involves so much fan energy—the fans have helped keep it real, as opposed to seeming beyond comprehension. "Usually at this scale, it feels bigger than you—like you can't relate to it," Kristen explains. "Well, I genuinely *do* relate to it. I like to share it with so many people all at the same time. We're remarkably lucky to get to feel that. It's like a club, and I'm so happy to be a member of the club." ■

(ABOVE LEFT) Kristen Stewart as the dying Bella from *Breaking Dawn - Part 1*. (ABOVE RIGHT) Kristen with Mackenzie Foy (Renesmee) in *Breaking Dawn - Part 2*.

FORKS HIGH SCHOOL HOME OF THE SPARTANS

FORKS HIGH

They don't sparkle. They don't drink blood. They don't phase. Bella's classmates may not get to participate in the *Twilight* movies' more otherworldly storylines, but for the actors who play "the humans," as they're affectionately (if generically) called, it didn't stop them from feeling central to the overall saga.

"The humans are vital to these films," says Michael Welch, who plays sweetly goofy Mike Newton. "First of all, we had to establish a base in reality for Bella, to represent normalcy and what her life could have been had she chosen to take a certain path. But we were also there to add levity, a break from the dark, intense things happening. So we were important, particularly in the first film. Beyond that, it became a comfort thing, a familiarity."

For Justin Chon, who plays Eric Yorkie, being the lighthearted part of the movie worked out perfectly. "It was cool for us, because as characters, you don't need to know what you don't know, so each movie was fun, because we got to see old friends, and it didn't require us to get so deep. Playing Eric was such a good time because he's a jokester." ➤

CAFETERIA   SC. 15 MEET ANGELA
                   PART A

21

Catherine Hardwicke in the humans' hangout, the cafeteria

➤ Christian Serratos loved playing "nice, wholesome, innocent" Angela Weber and recalls a lot of improvised joking around on the first film—encouraged by director Catherine Hardwicke—to help establish that easy, lighthearted camaraderie between them all. "We got to play around like real high school kids, which was cool," she says. "I even remember us having a miniature food fight that didn't make it in [*Twilight*]."

Michael recalls a few more details of that skirmish. "I think Christian threw a beet and then got yelled at, because that can really mess up a wardrobe," he says, laughing. "Someone else got hit in the face, I'm pretty sure."

Of course, they all loved working with Kristen Stewart, and Michael in particular credits her and Taylor Lautner for Mike's memorably funny quasi-then-queasy date scene with Bella and Jacob in *The Twilight Saga: New Moon*. "That was not originally going to be in the movie," says Michael. "But those two went to our director, Chris Weitz, and said, 'This is one of the funniest scenes in the book, you have to put this back in.' So they did, and I'm very grateful, because it was a blast, and that's my mark on American cinematic history at this point, throwing up in a movie theater. That was the most fun I had the whole series." ■

Anna Kendrick as
JESSICA STANLEY

Anna Kendrick says her favorite scene to shoot was the one that takes place outside a Port Angeles restaurant featuring her character, Jessica, and a suspiciously chummy Edward and Bella. "It was the last scene I shot on the first movie, and we were all tired and giddy at that hour, so it was hard to keep a straight face," recalls Anna. "But I think that ended up working for the scene, and Catherine [Hardwicke] used a take where I crack up a little."

Usually it's the people around Anna who burst into laughter, though, since the actress put her stamp on Bella's classmate as one of the series' funniest characters. "Anna's like a stand-up comedienne," says producer Wyck Godfrey, remembering how everyone was in stitches during filming of the *New Moon* scene when Jessica starts a rambling commentary after she and Bella leave the movie theater. "Every take the lines were different. We'd just go 'Okay, again!' And we'd all be laughing so hard because we had no idea what would come out. Then it proceeded to get more and more filthy, and even though we couldn't use any of it—because these are PG-13 films—we were having so much fun we did at least seven takes. It just speaks to her spontaneity and her quick brain."

Anna worked hard to make Jessica the kind of realistic, self-involved-yet-endearing friend audiences would recognize. Because she was one of the fortunate few to span the entire franchise, she saw how important it was to her fellow actors, too, to make the most of their characters. "Over time I noticed everyone becoming harder on themselves. The deeper we got into these movies, the more we understood how the fans felt about the books and the characters. I saw everyone's inner perfectionist."

When Anna received an Oscar nomination for her role in the 2009 film *Up in the Air*, it served to remind everyone of her dedication and talent. Michael Welch, meanwhile, saw it as a potential boon for himself and his fellow humans. "We couldn't have been more proud of her, but I'm not gonna lie, it definitely made me think, 'Is this going to get us in the movies a little more? And I'm usually standing next to her, so this is great for all of us!'" ■

THE MUSIC

What would *The Twilight Saga* motion pictures be without those exquisite marriages of song and scene? Music had to be essential, particularly when Stephenie Meyer thanks her favorite band, Muse, at the beginning of the novel BREAKING DAWN for "providing a saga's worth of inspiration."

Between the tastes of Stephenie Meyer, director Catherine Hardwicke, and celebrated music supervisor Alexandra Patsavas (*The OC, Gossip Girl*), the *Twilight* sound track offered a rich mixture of gifted artists from the indie rock scene. "There was already a vibe in place because Stephenie had created a music culture for fans because of her playlist, and she has a great love for alternative and indie rock," says Alex, who describes the goal of a sound track this way: "It has to be an incredibly listenable experience on its own, but it also has to be a companion to the movie. When a song and a scene are forever linked, that's when they're most effective."

Like the crisply rhythmic guitar charge of Muse's "Supermassive Black Hole" that matches the swooping athletic energy of the baseball scene perfectly. Or the way MUTEMATH, after viewing some footage, recorded the ideal song for when Edward and Bella show up together at school as an official couple, a rocker appropriately called "Spotlight." Though much of the *Twilight* sound track was previously released material—including the lilting Iron & Wine ballad "Flightless Bird, American Mouth" that Kristen Stewart suggested on set during shooting of the prom scene—bands like MUTEMATH and Paramore were brought in to get inspired to write an original song. Paramore's "Decode"—which played over the closing credits as a hard-driving voice to Bella's inner thoughts—even became the first single.

"That's when it's really interesting," says Alex about the opportunities afforded by a visit to the editing bay. "Because that's when the director and musicians are really speaking artist to artist."

Original contributions became a mantra after the multi-platinum success of the *Twilight* sound track, and it proved no problem, since submissions from labels and publishers hoping to be considered for *New Moon* poured in. "There was so much enthusiasm, not just from the music buyer but from bands and musicians, that we were able to ask for all unreleased materials," says Alex. "Of course, *New Moon* was a different movie—sad, somber—and the songs had to reflect that thematically." ➤

TWILIGHT SAGA PLAYLIST

Twilight

"Full Moon"—The Black Ghosts

"Eyes on Fire"—Blue Foundation

"Tremble for My Beloved"—Collective Soul

"I Caught Myself"—Paramore

"Never Think"—Rob Pattinson

"Spotlight [Twilight Mix]"—MUTEMATH

"Supermassive Black Hole"—Muse

"Go All the Way [Into the Twilight]"—Perry Farrell

"Flightless Bird, American Mouth"—Iron & Wine

"Decode"—Paramore

"Leave Out All the Rest"—Linkin Park

New Moon

"New Moon [The Meadow]"—Alexandre Desplat

"Monsters"—Hurricane Bells

"The Violet Hour"—Sea Wolf

"Satellite Heart"—Anya Marina

"Roslyn"—Bon Iver & St. Vincent

"Possibility"—Lykke Li

"I Belong to You [New Moon Remix]"—Muse

"Friends"—Band of Skulls

"Shooting the Moon"—OK Go

"Done All Wrong"—Black Rebel Motorcycle Club

"Hearing Damage"—Thom Yorke

"Slow Life"—Grizzly Bear featuring Victoria Legrand

"No Sound But the Wind"—Editors

"A White Demon Love Song"—The Killers

"Meet Me on the Equinox"—Death Cab for Cutie

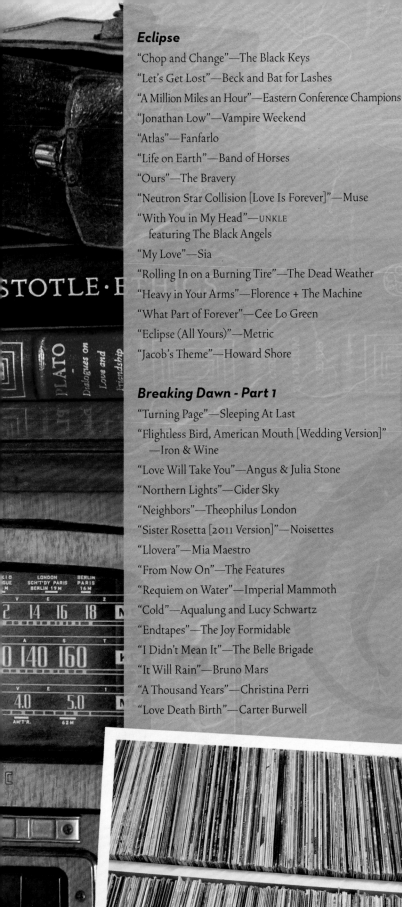

Eclipse

"Chop and Change"—The Black Keys

"Let's Get Lost"—Beck and Bat for Lashes

"A Million Miles an Hour"—Eastern Conference Champions

"Jonathan Low"—Vampire Weekend

"Atlas"—Fanfarlo

"Life on Earth"—Band of Horses

"Ours"—The Bravery

"Neutron Star Collision [Love Is Forever]"—Muse

"With You in My Head"—UNKLE
 featuring The Black Angels

"My Love"—Sia

"Rolling In on a Burning Tire"—The Dead Weather

"Heavy in Your Arms"—Florence + The Machine

"What Part of Forever"—Cee Lo Green

"Eclipse (All Yours)"—Metric

"Jacob's Theme"—Howard Shore

Breaking Dawn - Part 1

"Turning Page"—Sleeping At Last

"Flightless Bird, American Mouth [Wedding Version]"
 —Iron & Wine

"Love Will Take You"—Angus & Julia Stone

"Northern Lights"—Cider Sky

"Neighbors"—Theophilus London

"Sister Rosetta [2011 Version]"—Noisettes

"Llovera"—Mia Maestro

"From Now On"—The Features

"Requiem on Water"—Imperial Mammoth

"Cold"—Aqualung and Lucy Schwartz

"Endtapes"—The Joy Formidable

"I Didn't Mean It"—The Belle Brigade

"It Will Rain"—Bruno Mars

"A Thousand Years"—Christina Perri

"Love Death Birth"—Carter Burwell

➤ The results bore that out in what has been hailed as an alt-rock sound track classic. Bon Iver and St. Vincent's echoey folk duet "Roslyn" was like a moody lead-in for the breakup, while Swedish performer Lykke Li's "Possibility" played like a haunting swirl around a catatonic Bella, making it impossible not to feel her sadness. Radiohead's Thom Yorke proved to be a major get, contributing the brittle electronic track "Hearing Damage," which memorably accompanied Victoria being chased through the woods. "A lot of the songs in this movie were almost used as a score," says Alex, referring to the interplay between the artists' material and *New Moon* composer Alexandre Desplat's orchestral music. "The interaction between Desplat and the songs was rather seamless."

In an acknowledgment of that intertwining, for *Eclipse* composer Howard Shore and the band Metric collaborated on a track. Elsewhere, the third movie's grittiness dictated the chosen songs, from the Black Keys' blues-fuzzy "Chop and Change," which opens the movie, to UNKLE's driving "With You in My Head" setting the mood for a battle with the newborns. Plus, the *Twilight*/Muse connection gloriously came full circle as the band provided a new song, "Neutron Star Collision (Love Is Forever)," which became the first single.

The pairing of Beck with Bat for Lashes for the sexy "Let's Get Lost" reflected an interest in featuring duets. Says Alex, "They're an important throughline in our sound tracks, to have these male/female tracks, because of the love story."

By the time of *Breaking Dawn - Part 1*, the emphasis was on romance. "Beautiful songs, rather than wistful songs, and songs about love found," says Alex. Hence, the quietly plush "Turning Page" from Sleeping At Last, the swaying waltz and lyrical sentiment of Christina Perri's "A Thousand Years." Iron & Wine even re-recorded its "Flightless Bird, American Mouth" for the wedding scene, so the song could graduate from prom dance staple to nuptials standard. "It definitely felt grown up, a little more jazzy," says Alex. "Fans were so devoted to that band and song, I'm sure it's played at weddings all over the place."

Then there was cast member Mia Maestro, who had been working on her first album during filming of *Breaking Dawn* when she heard director Bill Condon wanted to use her "Llovera" over the honeymoon scene in *Part 1*. Mia was over the moon about it. "For him to say 'I really love this song,' and for Alexandra, who's a great music supervisor, to say 'It would be great to have Mia's song in it' was just really special."

Overall, Alex says it's been rewarding to work on a series of movies with such emotionally indelible characters and with an enthusiastic fan base that cares about music and appreciates being turned on to new and emerging artists. "I've been to so many *Twilight* events, and the bands have gotten such a great response," says Alex. "To watch the audience sing along a couple of weeks after the sound track is heady stuff, and moving."

She's hard at work assembling another powerful group of songs to join up with the saga's conclusion. "It's a little bit heartbreaking to know that there's ten to fifteen spots in a movie, and yet we have five hundred great songs," she says. "But these are fantastic problems to have." ■

THE CULLENS

I t's a brave teenage girl who finds out that gorgeous guy she likes to spend time with is a vampire, then agrees to meet a coven of them when he brings her home. But in Stephenie Meyer's world, the Cullens are exemplars of their kind: "vegetarian" vampires who value human life to a greater degree than their more bloodthirsty brethren do. They stick to feeding off animals (which gives their eyes a golden rather than scarlet hue) and take pains to engage with the human world through carefully created identities: a doctor and his wife, and a handful of high school—attending teens. What could be more normal? Yet in the realm of vampiredom, *normal* means something different.

"Normal vampires are nomadic and animalistic, and to fight that urge not to feed on humans, to live that vegetarian lifestyle, takes a lot more strength than to just give in to what your natural tendencies are," says Peter Facinelli, who plays father figure Dr. Carlisle Cullen. "I like that about them. It feels cool to be a Cullen. I feel lucky to be a part of that."

The Cullens play baseball together, hunt together, and, as things heat up with the welcoming of Bella into their fold, fight together. Theirs is a bond that seems to be too powerful to shatter. "They're a tight-knit family unit, and everybody wants that in their lives," says Jackson Rathbone, who plays Jasper Hale. "Whether you're born into it or try to achieve it with the family you make later in life, or even if it just becomes apparent with your friends that you're a group nothing can break, that's what's admirable about the Cullen family."

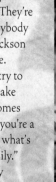

Living in wildlife-friendly Washington state, however—a necessity for an animal-centric diet—leads Peter to speculate that things might be easier for the Cullens if they'd just operate a critter farm in the backyard. "A rabbit would be a Snickers bar for them!" he jokes. ■

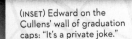

(INSET) Edward on the Cullens' wall of graduation caps: "It's a private joke."

PETER FACINELLI
LOOKS BACK

For the scene in *New Moon* in which Bella narrowly survives an attack by Jasper Hale, Dr. Carlisle has to tend the resulting wound. Peter Facinelli practiced his needle-and-thread skills for a month ahead of time to get ready. Early trials on Styrofoam didn't work—it didn't feel like flesh, Peter realized—so he moved to chicken breasts. Lots and lots of chicken breasts.

"I had a refrigerator full of stitched-up chicken breasts in my hotel room, and I thought, 'The housekeeper must think I'm really weird!'" recalls Peter. "Then I brought the chicken breasts [to the set] because I was really proud of myself, and I showed them to Kristen and said, 'Hey, I'm getting really good.' She looked at them and said, 'Yeah, I'd never let you stitch me up.' That was funny."

as

...LLEN

...s with potential Edward Cullens (including early favorite Jackson Rathbone) for Catherine Hardwicke's video camera in the run-up to principal photography on *Twilight*, but nobody opposite Kristen seemed to carry the requisite chemistry. Then London native Robert Pattinson's head shot on an executive's desk spurred a request for an audition tape, and before long Robert—whose biggest gig to date had been a small role in *Harry Potter and the Goblet of Fire*—had his own date to frolic with Kristen and Catherine.

There was some concern from higher-ups, though, about the actor's deliberately down-market look at the time: scraggly blond hair, rumpled clothes. Recalls Catherine, "They literally said, 'I don't see how you can make this guy look good.' And I said, 'He's going to start working out, we're going to cut his hair, change the color, he's getting a makeover, and he's going to look great!'"

Edward Cullen, after all, isn't your typical grungy teen. He's a moody romantic from another time—the early twentieth century, specifically—and his feelings about immortality are complicated, as lonely newcomer Bella Swan grasps after the truth comes out about who the object of her affection is. Privy to the psychological portrait Stephenie Meyer wrote of Edward in the unpublished manuscript for MIDNIGHT SUN, Robert approached Edward as a reluctant vampire struggling with whether he has a soul or not.

"He essentially thinks he doesn't, but at the same time doesn't have the courage to kill himself," Robert said in an interview before *Twilight* was released in 2008. "He's trying to find some kind of meaning. And when Bella arrives and he can have a connection with the living world again, it allows him to do that, and he can see and feel again through her." ➤

"FOOT BRIDGE" NO. 1

Catherine Hardwicke directs Robert Pattinson.

▣ PRODUCER'S TAKE

"I think back to the scene in *Twilight* when Edward first shows Bella his bedroom and starts to dance with her. Very early in the shooting, everything had been really dark and angsty and internalized between the two of them, and we all thought, 'Is this going to be completely joyless?' Rob's take on Edward is that he's self-loathing, morose, and that he can't possibly be with this woman because he'd want to kill her every minute of the day. The studio thought it might be a bit of a problem for fans who saw Edward as this knight in shining armor. But that scene, with his shy awkwardness showing her around, is very Rob. As good looking as he is, part of his charm is that he's a bit of a goofball, and the awkward way he gets her to dance with him was like magic. There's a lightness to it, yet it doesn't go broad. It's just enough to feel like a truly, authentically awkward moment. They pulled off something brilliant. Rob's essential qualities came through in that scene, and they're what make him a perfect Edward." —Wyck Godfrey

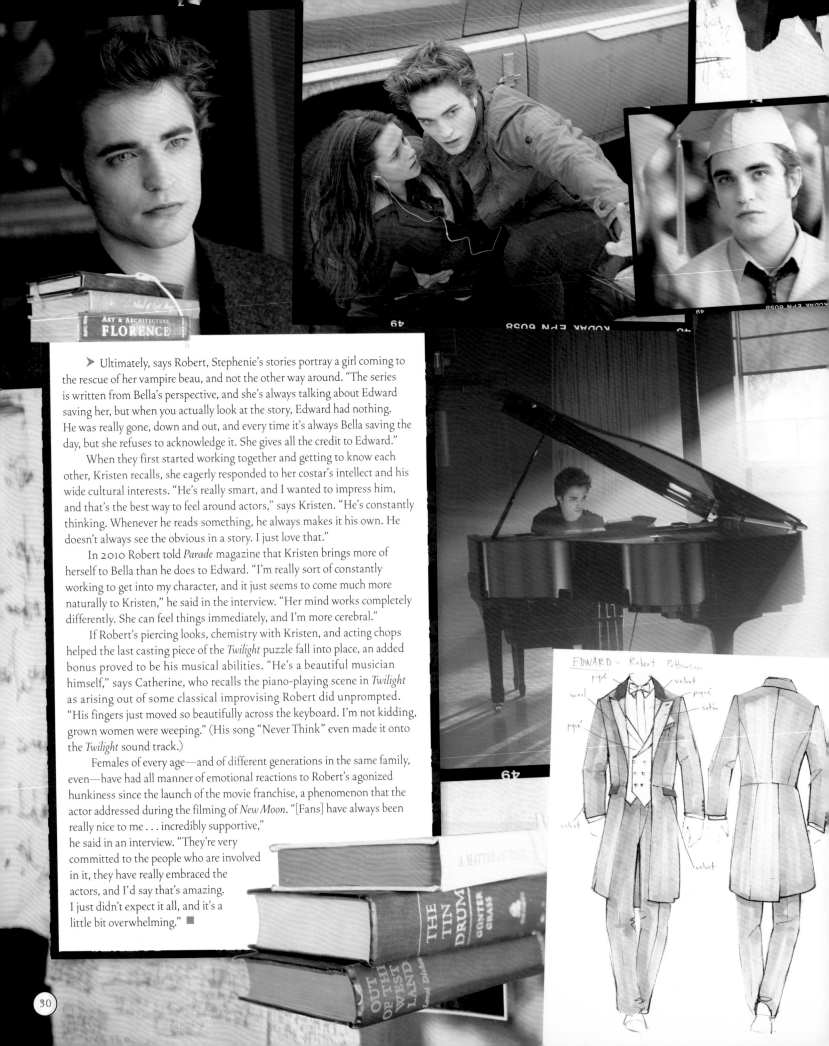

➤ Ultimately, says Robert, Stephenie's stories portray a girl coming to the rescue of her vampire beau, and not the other way around. "The series is written from Bella's perspective, and she's always talking about Edward saving her, but when you actually look at the story, Edward had nothing. He was really gone, down and out, and every time it's always Bella saving the day, but she refuses to acknowledge it. She gives all the credit to Edward."

When they first started working together and getting to know each other, Kristen recalls, she eagerly responded to her costar's intellect and his wide cultural interests. "He's really smart, and I wanted to impress him, and that's the best way to feel around actors," says Kristen. "He's constantly thinking. Whenever he reads something, he always makes it his own. He doesn't always see the obvious in a story. I just love that."

In 2010 Robert told *Parade* magazine that Kristen brings more of herself to Bella than he does to Edward. "I'm really sort of constantly working to get into my character, and it just seems to come much more naturally to Kristen," he said in the interview. "Her mind works completely differently. She can feel things immediately, and I'm more cerebral."

If Robert's piercing looks, chemistry with Kristen, and acting chops helped the last casting piece of the *Twilight* puzzle fall into place, an added bonus proved to be his musical abilities. "He's a beautiful musician himself," says Catherine, who recalls the piano-playing scene in *Twilight* as arising out of some classical improvising Robert did unprompted. "His fingers just moved so beautifully across the keyboard. I'm not kidding, grown women were weeping." (His song "Never Think" even made it onto the *Twilight* sound track.)

Females of every age—and of different generations in the same family, even—have had all manner of emotional reactions to Robert's agonized hunkiness since the launch of the movie franchise, a phenomenon that the actor addressed during the filming of *New Moon*. "[Fans] have always been really nice to me . . . incredibly supportive," he said in an interview. "They're very committed to the people who are involved in it, they have really embraced the actors, and I'd say that's amazing. I just didn't expect it all, and it's a little bit overwhelming." ■

TEAM EDWARD
WEIGHS IN

BELLA
I'm dying anyway. Every minute, I get closer, older --

EDWARD
That's how it's supposed to happen.

BELLA
Not the way Alice saw it. (off his sharp look) I heard her. She saw me like you.

EDWARD
Her visions change, Bella.

BELLA
Based on what someone decides. And I've decided.

He looks at her, angry. The fog envelops them.

EDWARD
Is that what you dream about? Becoming a monster?

BELLA
I dream about being with you forever.

EDWARD
You really want this?

BELLA
Yes.

He lowers his lips to her neck. One bite is all it would take.

EDWARD
You're ready right now?

BELLA
Yes.

His lips hover over her skin, a long beat... then he presses his lips to her throat. Not a bite. A kiss. He looks at her.

EDWARD
You're going to have a long and happy life with me. Isn't that enough?

She looks at him... and finally smiles.

BELLA
For now.

Robert Pattinson with *Breaking Dawn* director Bill Condon

"I feel really bad, because I feel like I'm the only person who's not politically correct and doesn't go both, but I'm Team Edward. So yeah, I think Team Edward, because Edward was the first one that was introduced, and I think I'm a very loyal person." —Judi Shekoni (Zafrina)

"I know it's kind of hard. Listen, when I was reading NEW MOON, I did get swayed momentarily, but just that initial impact of Edward was so strong, it's hard to let go of that! (Laughs) I think knowing Taylor as a person, it's hard for me to say Team Edward, because I love Rob, but I also love Taylor. I mean, at this point it's so connected to these adorable, wonderful boys, who I find so great. But based on the book alone, I would say Team Edward." —Bryce Dallas Howard (Victoria)

"You know what, I have a somewhat nuanced answer to this, which I know is obnoxious. But I've switched on this over the years. Originally I was Team Jacob, because Mike and I just hated Edward so much. But then I sort of went, 'You know what? This isn't about me, right? This is about Bella.' If I was a girl, then my criteria would be different, but I'm not, so I pick teams based on what's gonna be best for Bella, and clearly what's gonna make her happiest in life is to be with Edward. So I switched and I went to Edward, and then I kind of went back to Jacob for a little bit. Anyway, I finally landed on Team Edward, specifically for that criteria. It's what would make her happy. And if she's happy, I'm happy." —Michael Welch (Mike)

"Oh, man! You know, I have to be Team Edward, because I'm a vampire. I have to commit to that and be loyal. We are fiercely loyal about our covens." —Marlane Barnes (Maggie)

"I don't know, that Edward's quite the stud! They're both studs, but I'll go with Edward, because I care about Bella's happiness." —Bronson Pelletier (Jared)

"I will say that toward the end of *Breaking Dawn*, I started kind of swaying a little. Rob, man, he's getting kind of hunky! He's looking hunky to me! I think it was maybe that placenta and blood on his face that did it for me. You cannot ignore that commitment, man!" —Alex Meraz (Paul)

"I'm Team Edward. I have to be. I'm a vampire. I think the wolves have a real cool thing going. But I don't think Bella would make a good werewolf. She makes a *great* vampire, though." —Andrea Gabriel (Kebi)

THE EYES HAVE IT

Talk about irony: Vampires may have extrasensory powers in Stephenie Meyer's mythology, but for the actors who wore colored contacts to play them, their eyesight was anything but enhanced. "You could only see straight ahead," says Peter Facinelli, who plays Carlisle. "You had no peripheral vision."

Xavier Samuel, who plays Riley Biers in *The Twilight Saga: Eclipse*, describes it this way: "[The lenses] give you this tunnel vision, because all they are is a big block of red and a tiny hole to see through, and you've got them in for hours," he describes. "My eyes must have adjusted to that." Indeed, with the mass of new vampires joining *Breaking Dawn - Part 2*, the adjustment could get comical: Erik Odom, who plays nomad vamp Peter, recalls seeing people "wandering around bumping into each other with dazed looks on their faces."

On the plus side, many actors felt the lenses helped them transform mentally into character all but instantly. Christian Camargo, who plays gold-eyed Denali coven member Eleazar, explains, "You look at yourself in the mirror and suddenly your fantasy comes alive. I thought, 'Aha, this is what everyone's talking about!'" Volturi member Charlie Bewley (Demetri) corroborates: "You go into the contact-lens trailer, you put them in, and you become all the more dangerous and devilish. It really does sort of make the whole look pop."

Or, to put it another way: Cameron Bright, who plays Volturi member Alec, says his brother got one look at him and flatly said, "You're going to give me nightmares, man."

Forgetting to use the provided moisturizer, though, could make the removal process difficult. "A few times the contacts got so dried they stuck to my eyeballs," recalls Guri Weinberg, who plays Romanian vampire Stefan. "The technicians would have to spend another fifteen minutes lubricating each lens until they could get it off my eyeball."

Jackson Rathbone notes that even little Mackenzie Foy, who plays Renesmee Cullen, was affected but that she handled it like a champion. "[Her eyes] were bloodred, and involuntary tears were falling, and she just sat there with a determined smile on her face. She's the consummate professional at, like, what, ten years old?"

Co-producer Bill Bannerman sums up the experience of keeping five movies' worth of actors in good contact-lens spirits this way: "It's too bad kids aren't born with orange eyes." ■

One of the newborns in the human-hunting vampire's signature red contacts and pale makeup. "Vegetarian" vamps wore golden-hued contacts.

MAKEUP

Stephenie Meyer's vampires may sparkle like diamonds in the sun, but their everyday appearance when away from the rays is exceptionally pale, smooth, and flawless looking. On the first movie, the makeup for the vampires was a case of separating the Cullens from the humans without going overboard on paleness. But a considerable amount of white makeup in any form makes for lots of on-set correcting, especially if a vampire actor happens to touch his or her own skin accidentally.

On top of that, blue filters were applied in postproduction on *Twilight* that, while giving the movie's photography a cool, sleek look, seemed to highlight vampire makeup issues. Especially stressful was dealing with Robert Pattinson's beard. "At the end of the day, he's going to have five o'clock shadow," says production executive Gillian Bohrer. "There were scenes where it's particularly noticeable, and the blue color timing seemed to draw that out more."

The Cullens' porcelain beauty was less of a problem as the movies got away from the cerulean tint of *Twilight* and into earthier-hued cinematography on *New Moon* and *Eclipse*. And by the time shooting began for *The Twilight Saga: Breaking Dawn - Part 1* and *Part 2*, the directive was clear: Since contrasting vampires with humans was no longer as important, a more naturalistic pale look could be used.

For *Breaking Dawn* makeup director Jean Black, who was brought on at Robert Pattinson's suggestion (she had done his makeup for *Water for Elephants*), reducing actors' time in the cosmetic chair was essential. To that end, a special water-based spray makeup was applied that could be used with other products to give the right suggestion of attractive paleness without the excessive focus on white-makeup contouring that ate up time on previous movies. On Robert's face this worked wonders. "This allowed enough of his skin tone and natural indentations and contours of his face to come through," says Black, who also had to make sure everyone's looks stayed continuous with the other films in the saga.

There was still the wedding, though, in which plenty of humans would be there who needed to look different from vampires. *Breaking Dawn* cinematographer Guillermo Navarro came up with a special degraining treatment for the postproduction process, one Gillian wishes had been available for all the *Twilight* movies to reduce the amount of hand-wringing about makeup.

"It took away the grain in the Cullens' skin and just smoothed everything out and made them look a little more perfect," she explains. "The wedding was a great example, where we have a row of vampires who have all these perfect faces, and then you have a row of humans who just look human." ■

THE OUTDOORS

Give Catherine Hardwicke a nature-resplendent outdoor setting and she's happy, so in many ways, *Twilight*—with its Pacific Northwest–nesting vampires—was an ideal movie for a director who grew up hiking in Rocky Mountain National Park in Colorado. So many beautiful locations presented themselves to Catherine and her location scouts, from mossy, misty Oxbow Park in Portland (site of the "How long have you been seventeen?" conversation) to the rapturous views along the Columbia River Gorge, that she wanted moviegoers to feel about the outdoors the way she always has.

Says Catherine, "I want people to look at *Twilight* and go, 'Nature is beautiful. I should get out, away from my computer, and care about the natural world.'" Since then, it's becoming standard operating procedure for the filmmakers on *New Moon*, *Eclipse*, and the two parts of *Breaking Dawn* to take advantage of Mother Nature's bounty, whether it's been the verdant stretches outside of Vancouver in British Columbia (that meadow!) and the beaches on its coast, the ancient hill towns of Italy, or a magnificent waterfall in Brazil.

For Catherine on *Twilight*, it wasn't about getting beauty on camera at whatever cost, though. She wanted the production to care about the environment, too. Wooded locations where the vibrant green moss seemed especially prone to human trampling were used gingerly, whether it meant roping off areas or building special platforms for crew members to use. For the picturesque shots of Edward and Bella on moss-covered rocks by the water, a safety guy was in tow as well. "It was slippery and dangerous, and you could easily fall," says Catherine. "But it was a stunning location, and a beautiful scene." ➤

Catherine (to the left of the camera) insisted on platforms for the crew to stand on, to protect certain locations.

Catherine Hardwicke location-scouting, and acting out a possible scene for *Twilight*, at La Push

As for the thrilling vertical trip Edward takes "spider monkey" Bella on to the top of some massive firs, Catherine had her location-scouting work cut out for her. "If he's taking her to the top of these beautiful trees, there needs to be a ridiculous view," says Catherine. "So we were looking for a high point along the Columbia River Gorge that had a drop-off beyond it."

Thankfully, the location scouts hit upon the idea of contacting hang-glider enthusiasts in the area. Lo and behold, these soaring hobbyists knew of the place, a promontory where Robert Pattinson and Kristen Stewart could be filmed in close-up—without harnesses—on a specially built high platform near the edge of a cliff, a breathtaking view behind them. Then a second unit, in the forests of Silver Springs, Oregon—led by Andy Cheng—shot Rob's and Kristen's stunt doubles scurrying up a tree, attached to cables and pulled with winches, for the matching shots. "It was just an amazing setup to make that happen," says Catherine.

The quest to capture scenic beauty so enthralled Catherine that even when it came to scenes that could have easily been shot indoors, she took the fresh-air option. "The prom in the book is in the high school gym, and I'm like, 'No, no, no, that's not a beautiful, romantic, gorgeous location!'" And so the historic and quaint View Point Inn outside of Portland, located along—what else?—the vista-friendly Columbia River Gorge and featuring a charming gazebo, became another memorably picturesque outdoor location for *Twilight*'s emergent lovers. Adds Catherine, "I thought we could do so much better than a high school gym!" ▪

MIA MAESTRO LOOKS BACK

One actress who took full advantage of some of the breathtaking locations chosen for the *Twilight* movies was Mia Maestro, cast as Denali covenmate Carmen in *The Twilight Saga: Breaking Dawn - Part 1* and *Part 2*. The first day they shot in the snowy Canadian mountains that subbed for the Denalis' Alaskan home, Mia thought, "I've just landed in paradise."

She found it especially hard to leave Squamish, the small, woodsy town north of Vancouver that was the site of the Cullen house set. Though it was winter during filming, she wasn't permitted to downhill ski in her off time—you can't have your actors possibly breaking a leg—but she could cross-country ski, and after shooting wrapped she stayed behind. "I skied up to a lodge and stayed in this grove pine forest, where I was by myself, with no electricity. It was just beautiful!"

Billy Burke as
CHARLIE SWAN

Ask Billy Burke what he thinks fans of Charlie Swan respond to about the character, and it becomes obvious his answer stems from direct observation. "It depends on how old you are. If you're a fourteen-year-old girl, the general consensus is that everybody wants Charlie to be their dad. And if you're a fourteen-year-old girl's *mother*, you might look at it in a slightly different way," he says, laughing. "The response is still positive, nonetheless. I've been in this business almost twenty years now, and it's nice being a part of something that not only are people paying attention to, but people just seem to have such unabashed passion for."

Within the fandom, it's certainly not hard to find a substantial cheering section for Billy's nuanced turn as Bella's cop father, a stumbling single dad whose overprotectiveness masks a dry wit and a poignant guilt. "He's amazing," says Twilight Lexicon cofounder Lori Joffs. "He completely changed my impression of Charlie from the books. Charlie became funny, and an unforgettable character."

Billy says he found a latent humor in the *Twilight* script by Melissa Rosenberg, and that director Catherine Hardwicke let him run with it, which led to on-set inventions like the shotgun-cleaning gag. Eventually, Melissa's subsequent scripts infused Charlie's scenes with sarcastic touches. "She was using the colors I was bringing, and that was nice. Now, I don't know if he's that way in the books, but I feel fortunate that he evolved that way."

Much has been made of Billy's never having read the novels, but he insists there was reasoning behind it. "Charlie's pretty much oblivious the entire time until the final story," says Billy, referring to the saga's supernatural goings-on. "And since you can't un-know those things as an actor, I didn't know why I would need to know them." ➤

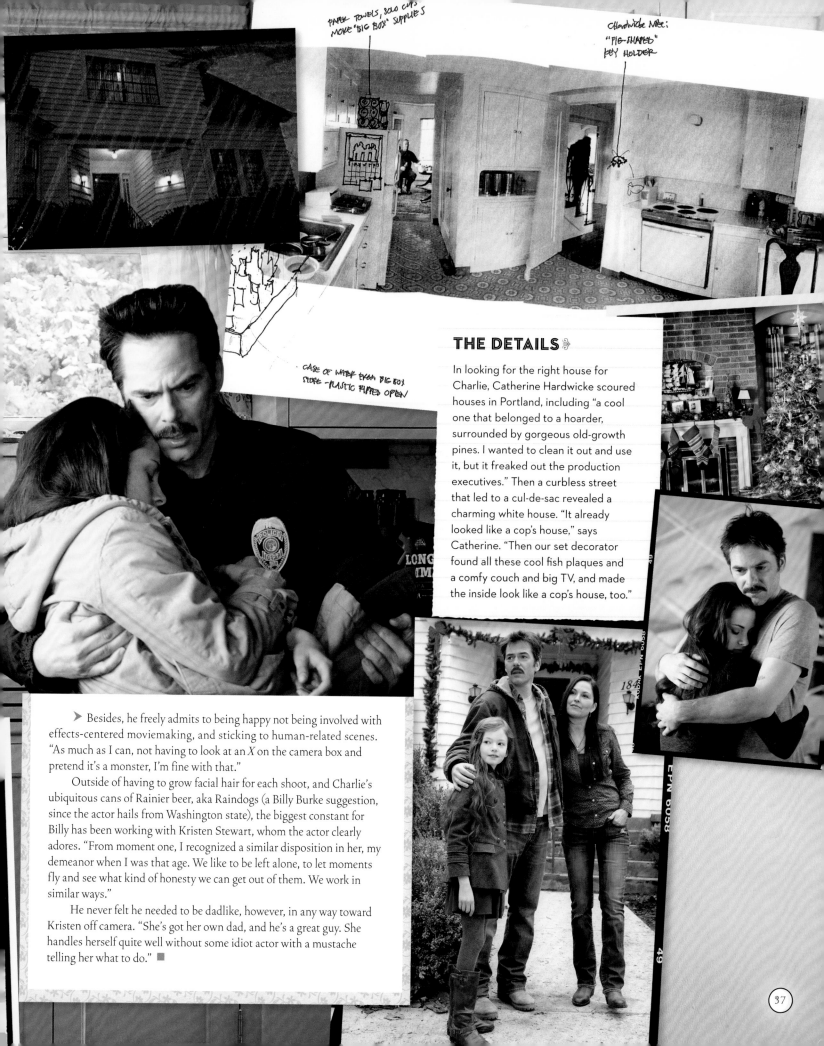

Handwritten notes:

PAPER TOWELS, SOLO CUPS
MAKE "BIG BOX" SUPPLIES

Hardwicke Note:
"PIG-SHAPED"
KEY HOLDER

CASE OF WATER FROM BIG BOX
STORE — PLASTIC RIPPED OPEN

THE DETAILS

In looking for the right house for Charlie, Catherine Hardwicke scoured houses in Portland, including "a cool one that belonged to a hoarder, surrounded by gorgeous old-growth pines. I wanted to clean it out and use it, but it freaked out the production executives." Then a curbless street that led to a cul-de-sac revealed a charming white house. "It already looked like a cop's house," says Catherine. "Then our set decorator found all these cool fish plaques and a comfy couch and big TV, and made the inside look like a cop's house, too."

➤ Besides, he freely admits to being happy not being involved with effects-centered moviemaking, and sticking to human-related scenes. "As much as I can, not having to look at an *X* on the camera box and pretend it's a monster, I'm fine with that."

Outside of having to grow facial hair for each shoot, and Charlie's ubiquitous cans of Rainier beer, aka Raindogs (a Billy Burke suggestion, since the actor hails from Washington state), the biggest constant for Billy has been working with Kristen Stewart, whom the actor clearly adores. "From moment one, I recognized a similar disposition in her, my demeanor when I was that age. We like to be left alone, to let moments fly and see what kind of honesty we can get out of them. We work in similar ways."

He never felt he needed to be dadlike, however, in any way toward Kristen off camera. "She's got her own dad, and he's a great guy. She handles herself quite well without some idiot actor with a mustache telling her what to do." ■

THE NOMADS

(ABOVE) Cam Gigandet (James), Edi Gathegi (Laurent), and Rachelle Lefevre (Victoria) are *Twilight*'s nomads.

Barefoot and bloodthirsty, the nomadic vampires in Twilight—James (Cam Gigandet), Laurent (Edi Gathegi), and Victoria (Rachelle Lefevre in *Twilight* and *New Moon*)—are the primal flip side to the Cullen family's do-no-human-harm philosophy. Operating outside the strictures of a coven, a nomad acts according to his or her own interests.

As Rachelle told the website Twilight Lexicon in 2008 about the flame-haired siren who roams with her vampire mate, James, "Victoria is like all of the parts we all have but don't like to admit. She's what we might all look like if we followed those nastier impulses."

Cam, whose character sets himself apart as the movie's central antagonist when he locks in on Bella at the Cullens' baseball game, says he took pride in the villain label. "I loved it," he says. "My character was the only one who actually got to fill out his instincts as a vampire. The [Cullens] had to squelch theirs!" ➤

(INSET) Storyboard art sketches out the emergence of the nomads.

(ABOVE) Cam, Edi, and Rachelle on the "magic carpet" that helps simulate vampire movement

In adapting TWILIGHT's inaugural meanies for the screen, however, a few changes were made. In a bit of color-blind casting, African American Edi Gathegi was chosen for Laurent, described in the book as "olive-toned." (Edi's memorable rejoinder in interviews was that he was a "black olive.") The "cropped hair" described in the book for James became a dirty blond, ponytailed look on Cam. And the nomads' frayed backpackers' garb was turned at Catherine Hardwicke's request into a stylishly rugged rock-and-roll ensemble, including bold colors, a jacketed yet shirtless look for Laurent that exposed a chiseled six-pack, and artfully arrayed accessories that represented keepsakes from their kills. Cam even regrets not walking away from filming with the souvenir of James's leather jacket—embroidered with badges like victims' trophies—if only to give to his dad, who keeps a shrine to his movie-star son in his office. "It's got *Twilight* memorabilia," he says. "But it wouldn't matter what I was in. He's a dad."

The irony that accompanies being fearful of the nomads is, of course, that they're the typical vampires, the everyday hunters. Says Edi, "We thirst for human blood. We're natural predators, so that's what we have to eat in order to survive, whereas the Cullens are slightly more evolved."

To the nomads, the Cullens are the crazy ones, possibly shame filled and weak, and therefore ripe for punishment. "Here is a group of vampires who are maintaining these human confines, these mortal societal rules, and it's very strange to the three of us," Rachelle explains. "So not only are they this family, which is bizarre, but they have a human in their midst."

Cam has especially fond memories of working with Rachelle. "We had such a good time together," says Cam. "She was an amazing actress, one of those people [who's] easy to be around, who makes the entire set enjoyable."

Being a nomad, though, was especially cool, he notes. "There was really no limit. We let our imaginations run wild and just dove in, and it was fun that the three of us got to do it together." ■

CAM GIGANDET LOOKS BACK

It's one of the more iconic moments in *Twilight*: the sight of three vastly different-seeming vampires emerging from the misty forest to see what the Cullens are up to. Then they realize there's a delectable human in their midst, and the mood becomes infinitely more threatening. "That was one of the scenes where we really got to portray that to these vampires, humans are really just snacks," says Cam, referring to the memorable descriptor for Bella that Stephenie—and then screenwriter Melissa Rosenberg—put in James's mouth. "Even though we were freezing and we were barefoot, that memory sticks in my mind. That was a good moment."

And what was the aroma he imagined Bella gave off? "You know, at the time I was probably so cold I wasn't thinking about anything other than hot chocolate and some macaroni and cheese," he says. "I'm sure those came into my mind."

FAN BITES: THE FRENZY BEGINS
Twilight Mania

Movie studios have come to learn a lot about the anticipation level for their upcoming releases by going to Comic-Con or setting up a publicity tour. And though Summit surely wouldn't have made a movie of TWILIGHT if they didn't think moviegoers would go, what they came to realize was that there are moviegoers, and then there are Twilight fans.

The normally geek boy–heavy gathering at Comic-Con in San Diego saw a decidedly different gender demographic surge on July 24, 2008, when 6,500 fans of Stephenie Meyer's books overwhelmed Hall H at the San Diego Convention Center for the afternoon panel with Stephenie, director Catherine Hardwicke, and stars Kristen Stewart, Robert Pattinson, Taylor Lautner, Rachelle Lefevre, Cam Gigandet, and Edi Gathegi. Summit production executive Gillian Bohrer remembers how, before the panel even started, a slow build in appreciative audience shrieks could be heard with each name card placed on the long, empty table. "Then they introduced the actors, and by the time they got to Rob, the screaming reminded me of Beatles footage," says Gillian, who called producer Wyck Godfrey during the session so he could hear the decibel level through the phone. "Throughout the panel, the screaming never stopped."

"We were all just treated like mega rock stars," recalls Catherine. "It was so funny and fun, everyone going so crazy. It was almost like you had a contact high with the audience. I've never been in that kind of rarefied air."

Patrick Wachsberger, then Summit's co-chairman, says, "That's when we all realized we had something really, really unique."

Certainly the media took notice that day. "The Shrieks Beat the Geeks" was the headline in *The Hollywood Reporter*'s coverage, while Jen Yamato, covering Comic-Con for the movie website Rotten Tomatoes, captured a growing mood with the simple declaration, "It's official; *Twilight* . . . is a phenomenon in the making."

And yet it wasn't entirely apparent to Summit just how big things could still get that first year. In November, a mall tour was planned with the principal cast, arranged with the clothing store Hot Topic, where signings would take place. Rob was slated to make five solo appearances; Kristen would do a few with Nikki Reed; and Taylor, Rachelle, and Edi would make joint appearances at five other locations around the country. But as word spread through the Internet about the chance to see *Twilight* talent in person, little did Summit or Hot Topic or the stars know that prerelease excitement was about to reach frenzy levels. ➤

SUMMIT ENTERTAINMENT PRESENTS
"THE TWILIGHT EXPERIENCE"
A ONE-NIGHT-ONLY SPECIAL THEATRICAL RE-RELEASE OF GLOBAL SENSATION
TWILIGHT
FEATURING AN INTRODUCTION BY MEMBERS OF THE CAST
READING-GASLAMP THEATER 701 5TH AVENUE
THURSDAY, JULY 23RD
DOORS OPEN AT 5:30 P.M.
FANS WITH TICKETS WILL BE ADMITTED ON A FIRST-COME, FIRST-SERVE BASIS
SOLD OUT

Screenings of *Twilight* at Comic-Con 2008. The cast came to introduce the film.

> **❝** When we went to that first Comic-Con, I was in the audience with the producers. The panel was Catherine, Stephenie, and the cast. We were in the audience already, thinking, 'Wow, this is cool. There's five thousand people here. Or more.' And at one point, before it starts, this little girl came up to me and she asked me to sign her book. I was shocked. I said, 'How do you know who I am?' She leans over and says, very seriously, 'I know who you are.' That was very 'Wow.' No one knows who the screenwriter is, you know? **❞**
>
> —MELISSA ROSENBERG (SCREENWRITER, *THE TWILIGHT SAGA*)

The first stop was San Francisco, at the Stonestown Galleria, and though pre-event stipulations idealistically asked for lining up to begin no earlier than 6 A.M. for the five hundred or so people that organizers assumed would be the high end of attendee numbers, *Twilight* fever dictated a much more rabid response.

"I get asked, when did I know *Twilight* was going to be big?" says Summit regional publicity and promotions director Sabryna Phillips. "Well, it was when I got the four A.M. phone call that there were already a thousand fans in line in San Francisco."

Although an unplanned free-for-all of eager fans crowding the mall entrance doors led to a brief shutdown of the event until organizers could rethink the logistics of Rob's appearance—and all appearances afterward—a message had been sent loud and clear: no more mall tours. Okay, *two* messages: *Twilight* was off and running, and life would never be the same for not just a handsome if bewildered lad from England who had to get used to being called "Edward," but for everyone who would ever be involved with the *Twilight* movies, thanks to a bountiful, exuberant fan base.

"It never ceases to surprise me over the course of the whole *Twilight Saga* how dedicated the fans have been," says Nancy Kirkpatrick, president of worldwide marketing at Summit Entertainment. "Some of those at that first *Twilight* tour are still coming out to all our various events now. It's wonderful seeing how happy it makes people, how it brings them together."

PATRICK BRENNAN
LOOKS BACK

Since *The Twilight Saga* exploded, conventions have sprung up across the globe, bringing in actors from the films for question-and-answer sessions, parties, contests, photo ops, and all manner of fan socializing. Patrick Brennan, cast as Irish coven vampire Liam in *The Twilight Saga: Breaking Dawn - Part 2*, shares his thoughts on the highs and lows:

"I've been to a ton of these *Twilight* conventions—Nashville, Boston, Dallas, Orlando, England, Germany—and it's a ride," says Patrick. "You walk out onstage and they're screaming and you don't really understand why. They haven't seen the movie. I guess they've read the books and know the character. I'm not going to lie, it feels pretty good. They're the greatest fans on the planet. It's touching to feel all the warmth and love. Of course, then you go home and you've got to do dishes and people don't pay attention to you. It's a tough pill to swallow. You're treated like a god for three days and you get home and you're completely invisible. I don't know if my wife likes sharing her husband like that."

Complications

Chris Weitz directs Kristen Stewart and Rob Pattinson in the meadow.

DIRECTOR'S JOURNAL

CHRIS WEITZ AND *NEW MOON*

Thematically, if the first novel in the TWILIGHT series is about the "fascination and intrigue" that comes with first love, says director Chris Weitz, then NEW MOON is the sufferer's lament. "It deals more with heartbreak and longing. I mean, it's what is perceived by the readership, probably, as the most horrible breakup in history—forget about Antony and Cleopatra, this is the one! But then it's the rapture of being reunited toward the end."

Chris's ideas for *The Twilight Saga: New Moon* ensured that the franchise wouldn't rest on the laurels of what made the first film a hit. "It would be interesting to take what in Catherine Hardwicke's very successful version was a quick-cutting, dynamic, sort of kinetic cool feeling and turn it into a very romantic, in some ways deliberately paced, wide-screen romance," says Chris. "To take it very epic. That led to working with cinematographer Javier Aguirresarobe, because his style is very much about beauty and light and warmth."

For the overall color scheme in *New Moon*, Chris and Javier sought earthy lushness, saving certain hues for big moments. "We knew we wanted to keep away from red, because we wanted people's eyes to just get used to not seeing it, so when you finally see red in Montepulciano at the end, in that square en masse, it really has this visual punch. So we kept to earth tones, greens, browns, and grays, and we stayed away from the first movie's cooler colors. And Vancouver has a very beautiful neutral-lighting environment." ➤

Bella's bureau

David Brisbin, Stephenie Meyer, Wyck Godfrey, and Meghan Hibbett

• PRODUCER'S DIARY •

Producer Wyck Godfrey believes NEW MOON was the most difficult of the books to bring to the screen because the emotional stakes sideline one major figure and bring another to the forefront. "Edward's gone, Bella's depressed, and it was the introduction of the werewolves," says Wyck. "There is Team Edward and Team Jacob for a reason, and fans really wanted the wolves to be everything they envisioned in their minds, so how do you do that?"

The answer is, you hire a director who knows something about computer-generated animals being integrated into a human story, as director Chris Weitz became in the wake of the Oscar-winning fantasy epic *The Golden Compass*. As Wyck explains, "He's somebody who came from writing and storytelling on a more intimate scale, so he was really able to capture not only the intimacy of Bella's loneliness but also the more expansive parts of the movie."

Those "expansive parts" included hauling the production to the hills of Tuscany in Italy for the film's climax. "Chris is a very cultured person himself, so with the introduction of the Volturi, and their ancient, civilized Renaissance world, he was able to have immediate opinions about how to handle it, and he did it to great effect."

Also invaluable, adds Wyck, was Chris's love of actors. "He's acted himself, he's respectful of the process, so he's much more precise and articulate about communicating the intent of each scene. He's a calm presence on set, and it was really good for Kristen, because she was without Rob and Taylor for a lot of the emotional scenes. So that bubble Chris put around her, so just he and she could communicate to get her to those darker places, was really important."

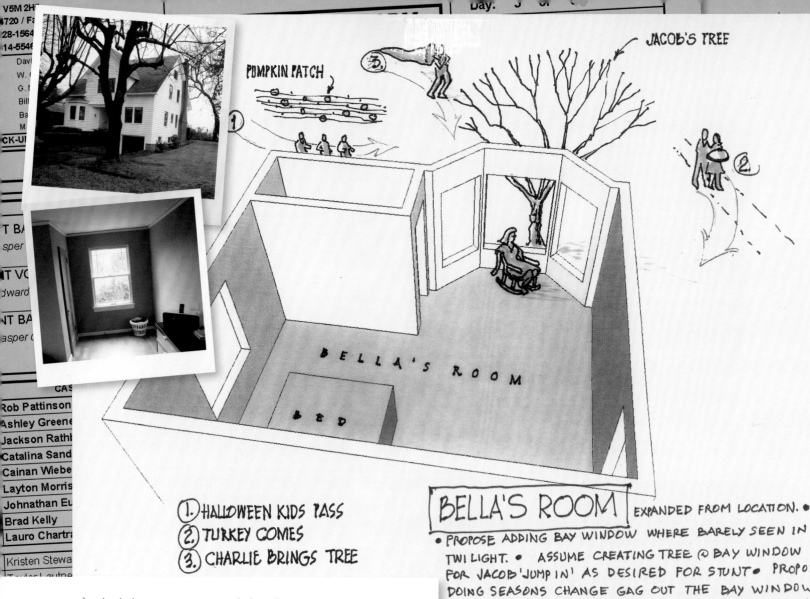

PUMPKIN PATCH

JACOB'S TREE

BELLA'S ROOM

BED

① HALLOWEEN KIDS PASS
② TURKEY COMES
③ CHARLIE BRINGS TREE

BELLA'S ROOM EXPANDED FROM LOCATION. •
• PROPOSE ADDING BAY WINDOW WHERE BARELY SEEN IN
TWILIGHT. • ASSUME CREATING TREE @ BAY WINDOW
FOR JACOB 'JUMP IN' AS DESIRED FOR STUNT • PROPOSE
DOING SEASONS CHANGE GAG OUT THE BAY WINDOW
UTILIZING 3 DIRECTIONS; A POSSIBLE CONFIG. SHOWN •

➤ The darker tones were particularly well suited to him personally, says the director. "I'm not much fun and also kind of brooding, personally," he jokes.

But it led to one of the franchise's signature moments, the visualization of Stephenie's ingenious textual manifestation of Bella's lost seasons, when page after page is blank except for the months. "That's very true to one's sense of time going by but nothing is gained when you're heartbroken," says Chris, who used his knowledge of motion-control camera work from *The Golden Compass* to create a 360-degree shot that circles a catatonic Kristen Stewart—and all the while the background changes to indicate the passage of much time. He credits visual effects supervisor Susan MacLeod with bringing all seven layers of the shot together. "I think it's a great example of how you can use something like CGI [computer-generated imagery], which is generally used for big explosions or robots, to actually express something emotional."

Chris expresses relief in looking back at how *New Moon* survived losing one of its key characters for a huge stretch. His worry even led him to imagine a subplot for the missing Edward. "I came up with the stupidest idea ever, where Edward goes and works at Mother Teresa's house of the dying in Calcutta." He laughs at the memory of broaching the notion with Stephenie. "She very kindly suggested that maybe it didn't fit in."

He did manage to get in a little personal career reference elsewhere, however. "Bella's compass is golden," notes Chris. "That was one of my little jokes." ∎

Wyck Godfrey, Kristen Stewart, and Chris Weitz on the set in Italy

"I really enjoy anything that the wolves are in. I think they did an amazing job with the graphics. Every time I see a wolf I get really excited, and it just makes me realize how much of a fan I actually became of the books." —**Christian Serratos (Angela)**

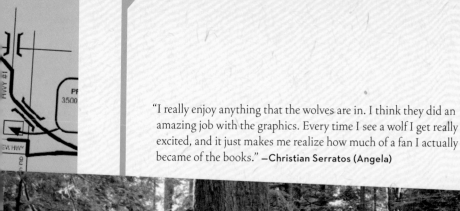

"At the premieres, when I watch the movies, every single scene in which Taylor takes his shirt off is my favorite, because every girl in the place starts going crazy, and when I look over at him, you can see him just shrink down in his seat a little bit, and I just start laughing. Not laughing at him, but laughing at the fact that I'm so glad I'm not in his position."
—**Cameron Bright (Alec)**

(RIGHT) Alex Meraz, Kiowa Gordon, Chaske Spencer, Taylor Lautner, Tyson Houseman, and Bronson Pelletier: the wolf-pack actors

"I really sort of gravitate toward the wolf stuff; maybe it's because I'm envious. They're tan, and they don't have to deal with the wigs and the white makeup and all that crazy stuff. They just sort of jump all around each other. I don't know, there's something really attractive about a bunch of shirtless dudes. But there's a warmth, an interaction between them." —**Nikki Reed (Rosalie)**

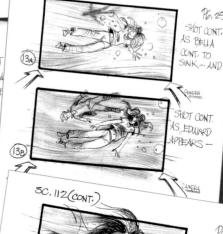

SC. 111 (CONT.)   Pg.10

⑩ CUT TO: EDWARD: "STOP THIS NOW, BELLA."

⑪ CUT TO: BELLA: "YOU WON'T STAY WITH ME ANY OTHER WAY."

FROM **PAGE** TO **SCREEN**

ADAPTING NEW MOON

When it came to writing the screenplay for *The Twilight Saga: New Moon*, Melissa Rosenberg readily admits it was the hardest of Stephenie Meyer's tetralogy to adapt. "In the first movie, you've established Rob Pattinson as your romantic lead, and then in the second movie you basically lose him for a good third of the movie. Gone."

With Edward on a guilt-ridden sabbatical, our heroine has entered into a rootless despair. "All of her drive, everything that happens to her in the second act while he's gone, which is sixty pages, is all motivated by someone who's not there," says Melissa. One solution, then, was to make the moments in the novel when Bella's subconscious conjures her missing beau's voice into visual manifestations of Edward—hence, more Rob Pattinson. And because this is an apparition Bella can see, Melissa could turn what was a moment of internal comfort in the novel—Bella realizing that Edward's voice is still with her, which prevents her from engaging with a group of strange men at a bar—into a more dangerous, dynamic rendering of pain and loss. "It's a misguided attempt to change things for herself, but it's active," says Melissa. ▶

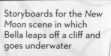

Storyboards for the *New Moon* scene in which Bella leaps off a cliff and goes underwater

Emboldened by the way she'd tied certain elements together in *Twilight*, Melissa looked to do the same with a key plot point in *New Moon*: Edward's mistaken interpretation of Harry Clearwater's funeral. "When it came to Harry's heart attack, rather than have that be natural causes, it seemed a great way to tie Charlie into the story. Harry's on the hunt for wolves, and Victoria actually causes the heart attack right there and then. Since his funeral is such an instigator, the whole reason we go to the Volturi in the third act, I wanted to weight it with emotion, to see Harry go through that."

Throughout the process, says Melissa, Stephenie was "a terrific collaborator. The mythology is the mythology, and you don't mess with the mythology—it's a detailed world, and it's an amazing thing she's come up with. But after she read my first draft of *Twilight*, she realized I wasn't going to butcher her child. In no way would she have not allowed for my voice." ∎

```
EXT. WOODS - DUSK

Edward stops by a fallen tree. Turns to Bella.

                    EDWARD
          We need to leave Forks.

                    BELLA
          What? Why?

                    EDWARD
Carlisle's supposed to be ten years older than he looks;
          people will start noticing.

                    BELLA
          Okay, when?

                    EDWARD
          Now.

Bella reels, trying to take this in. Finally --

                    BELLA
     I'll have to think of something to tell Charlie,
          but I can -- (beat) When you say "we" --

                    EDWAR
          I mean my fami

                    BELLA
          (stunne
What? -- no -- Edward, what happ
              nothin

                    EDWAR
You're right -- it was nothing
expected. Nothing compared to wha
          You don't belong

                    BELL
          I belong

                    EDWAR
          You don'

                    BELL
          -- I'm com

                    EDWAR
Bella -- (beat; deliberately) I d
```

Chris Weitz with Taylor Lautner on NEW MOON

Taylor Lautner as
JACOB BLACK

Taylor Lautner remembers exactly what struck him about the character of Jacob Black, and it's the same feeling he gets from fans in love with the shape-shifting Quileute who turned Stephenie Meyer's epic love story into something more complicated than just vampire-meets-girl. "Jacob's about as loyal as they come," says Taylor. "Everything he's gone through, everything he's had to put up with, in the end, he's still one hundred percent loyal to Bella, whether it's romantically or as a friend. He will always be there for her no matter what, and I think it's what the fans—and certainly I—responded to most about him."

The marked change in Jacob from *Twilight* to *Breaking Dawn* was part of the appeal in playing him, too. "In *Twilight* he's just a boy, this happy-go-lucky, friendly boy, and through the emotional journey he goes on, from his fight for Bella to the fight with his own wolf pack, he really does become a man in *Breaking Dawn*."

He's also, according to the novels, a much larger presence—story-wise and physically—from first book to second book, so while Taylor was shooting *Twilight*, he tried not to allow himself to get too excited about the prospect of *New Moon* getting made. "I remember thinking, I need to focus on Jacob right now, and just take it one step at a time," he says. "But in the back of my mind, I was excited to explore that side of Jacob."

So while the movie executives played the waiting game until the release of *Twilight*—hoping reaction would be strong enough to continue the franchise (yes, fans, they truly didn't know)—Taylor wasn't taking any chances: He started his own "phasing," you could say. "As soon as I finished filming, I came back home and knew I had a lot of work ahead of me. I started hitting the gym five, six days a week, and read the books over and over again, studying the character and how much he transforms emotionally." ➤

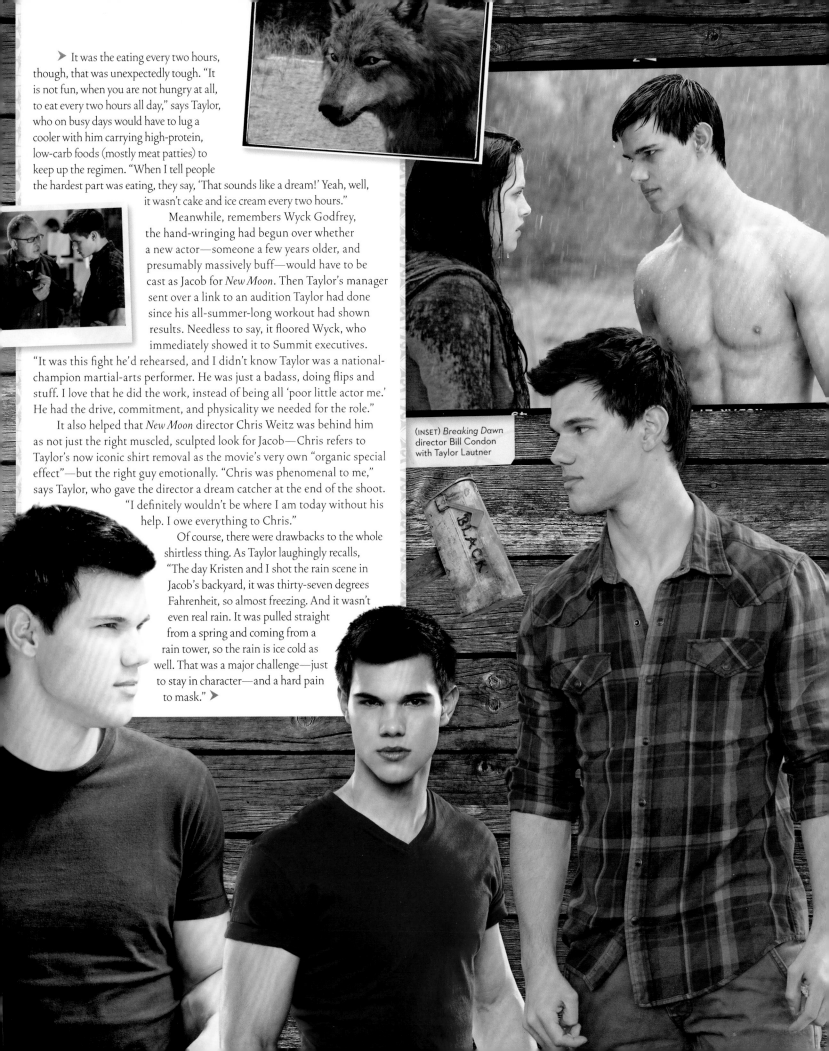

➤ It was the eating every two hours, though, that was unexpectedly tough. "It is not fun, when you are not hungry at all, to eat every two hours all day," says Taylor, who on busy days would have to lug a cooler with him carrying high-protein, low-carb foods (mostly meat patties) to keep up the regimen. "When I tell people the hardest part was eating, they say, 'That sounds like a dream!' Yeah, well, it wasn't cake and ice cream every two hours."

Meanwhile, remembers Wyck Godfrey, the hand-wringing had begun over whether a new actor—someone a few years older, and presumably massively buff—would have to be cast as Jacob for *New Moon*. Then Taylor's manager sent over a link to an audition Taylor had done since his all-summer-long workout had shown results. Needless to say, it floored Wyck, who immediately showed it to Summit executives. "It was this fight he'd rehearsed, and I didn't know Taylor was a national-champion martial-arts performer. He was just a badass, doing flips and stuff. I love that he did the work, instead of being all 'poor little actor me.' He had the drive, commitment, and physicality we needed for the role."

It also helped that *New Moon* director Chris Weitz was behind him as not just the right muscled, sculpted look for Jacob—Chris refers to Taylor's now iconic shirt removal as the movie's very own "organic special effect"—but the right guy emotionally. "Chris was phenomenal to me," says Taylor, who gave the director a dream catcher at the end of the shoot. "I definitely wouldn't be where I am today without his help. I owe everything to Chris."

Of course, there were drawbacks to the whole shirtless thing. As Taylor laughingly recalls, "The day Kristen and I shot the rain scene in Jacob's backyard, it was thirty-seven degrees Fahrenheit, so almost freezing. And it wasn't even real rain. It was pulled straight from a spring and coming from a rain tower, so the rain is ice cold as well. That was a major challenge—just to stay in character—and a hard pain to mask." ➤

(INSET) *Breaking Dawn* director Bill Condon with Taylor Lautner

▶ Filming the birth scene in *The Twilight Saga: Breaking Dawn - Part 1* was a different kind of grueling. "From the beginning, just trying to keep Bella alive, through to the moment that I believe she is truly dead, and I go outside and lose it all, that as a whole was definitely the most emotional scene for me. And we didn't shoot it in little tiny pieces, so that really helped. We shot from beginning to end, so as intense as it looked in the movie, it felt just that intense in the room."

Off camera, Taylor made the most of his downtime by cheering up the cast and crew, impressing everyone with his ability to catch a grape in his mouth tossed from almost any distance, and dog-sitting for a few cast members. "He volunteered a couple of times, which was so nice," says Mia Maestro, who plays Carmen in the *Breaking Dawn* movies, and who had her wheaten terrier, River, with her during filming in Canada.

"It's hard for me not to like a dog," reveals Taylor, who has also kept time with Nikki Reed's and Kristen's pooches. Mia's, though, started out adorable, then showed a different side. "It looked at first like this little cute dog, then it was just me and the dog in my trailer, and it was standing at attention, staring at me, like it was watching every move I made. Then it would start barking at me randomly, and I was getting a little nervous. Mia's dog was funny. It might have been a guard dog!"

Hmm, a creature that initially seems cute but might prove to be a little dangerous . . . sound familiar, Team Jacob fans? ■

Bill Condon, BREAKING DAWN cinematographer Guillermo Navarro, and Taylor Lautner

ON BELLA, no longer shaking. Her eyelids are losing the fight against sleep. INCLUDE JACOB, spooned behind her, resting on one elbow, facing Edward across the tent. Edward glares at him.

                    EDWARD
     Get Bella out of your little fantasies, dog. Or we're going to
                 have a problem.

                    JACOB
     Payback for listening to my thoughts.

                    EDWARD
     Trust me, I'd shut you out if I could.

                    JACOB
     I really get under that ice-cold skin of yours, don't I? What,
             you doubting her feelings for you?

ON BELLA - Her eyes flicker open slightly. The guys don't see she's awake. When Edward doesn't answer, Jacob scoffs --

                    JACOB
     Nice. Picking through *my* brain's okay, but letting me into *yours*,
                 forget it.
                 (no response)
     Look. I know she's in love with you --

                    EDWARD
     -- Good --

                    JACOB
     -- But she's in love with me, too. She just won't admit it to
                 herself.

                    EDWARD
                 (long beat)
     I can't tell you if you're right.

Jacob's taken aback by his honesty. Beat.

                    JACOB
     Then let me ask you something. If she chooses me --

                    EDWARD
     She won't --

                    JACOB
     -- *If* she did. Would you try to kill me?

ON BELLA - she waits for the answer.

▣ PRODUCER'S TAKE

"In some ways, Taylor brings the biggest smile to my face. Of all the scenes we shot with him, the one that made me so proud of him and impressed me with his commitment and work ethic was in *The Twilight Saga: Eclipse* where he has to run Kristen up the mountain carrying her, then stop and have a whole conversation while she's in his arms. And it has to be effortless for him, because Jacob is superhumanly strong, yet it's a very emotional conversation. Well, we had rigged this thing—basically a dolly with her butt in it—that we could shoot while he walked along with her so that it looked effortless. But it just didn't work. It didn't look good. So Taylor said, 'I'll just do it.' Even someone as light as Kristen, you could imagine holding someone for a three-page-long dialogue scene, walking from eight in the morning until four in the afternoon. You can't even see him huffing and puffing. We were in awe of him physically. None of us could believe he pulled it off, and by the end of the day, his biceps would just give. You could see it on his face. But there are maybe one percent of the actors in the universe who would have done what he did. Most would have said, 'You know what? Call me when that thing is fixed. I have to figure out how to do this role.' But Taylor was just amazing." —Wyck Godfrey

TEAM JACOB
WEIGHS IN

"I always say Team Bella, which is actually true. I'm on Bella's side. Although I'm a Jacob myself. I'm not an Edward." —Chris Weitz

"I'm gonna make up my mind now. Because I've been saying Team Switzerland for the longest time, but I think I just need to pick, you know? I think Team Jacob, because he's the underdog, and I relate with that. I relate with not being the one who's chosen." —Justin Chon (Eric)

Taylor Lautner and Mackenzie Foy

"Team Jacob! That's my boy!"
—Chaske Spencer (Sam)

"It's not just my character, he is my son! I am the lineage of the werewolf! I've got to go Team Jacob all the way." —Gil Birmingham (Billy)

"Yeah, I mean, I gotta stick with the pack."
—Tyson Houseman (Quil)

"I'm the most loyal Team Jacob person on the planet. Team Jacob saved my ass, so I can't separate."
—Julia Jones (Leah)

Robert Pattinson, Taylor Lautner, Kristen Stewart, and Christie Burke, who plays Renesmee in Alice's vision of the future

WHO'S WHO:
THE WOLF PACK

A significant aspect to creating the computer-generated wolves for the *Twilight* movies was giving them the requisite differentiating features—coloring, size—that made Jacob-wolf stand apart from Sam-wolf, and so on. As *The Twilight Saga: Breaking Dawn - Part 2* visual effects supervisor Terry Windell explains, "You have to have a sense of the character so they don't all become the same." As the designs were refined from movie to movie, the actors' wolf counterparts came into their own as characters. "Take Jacob. When he's a wolf, he isn't just a hairy beast. He's still the third member of your lead triangle." ■

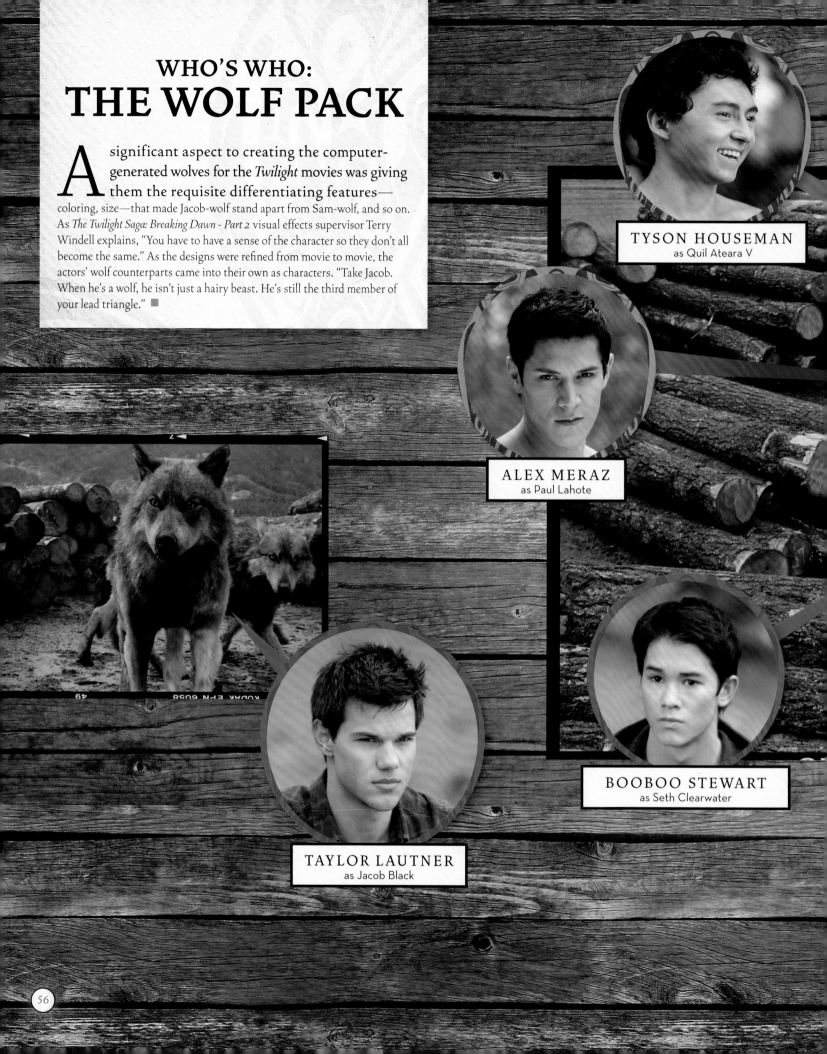

TYSON HOUSEMAN
as Quil Ateara V

ALEX MERAZ
as Paul Lahote

BOOBOO STEWART
as Seth Clearwater

TAYLOR LAUTNER
as Jacob Black

KIOWA GORDON

BRONSON PELLETIER
as Jared Cameron

ASKE SPENCER
as Sam Uley

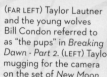

BODIES IN MOTION:
THE WOLF-PACK PHYSIQUE

Shape-shifters run hot, with "hot" meaning one thing for the characters—that's 108 degrees of body temperature for each wolf in the pack—and another for moviegoers who've swooned to the sculpted physiques on display from *New Moon* on. From the first appreciative screams heard when Jacob tended to an injured Bella by taking off his shirt, it was clear that Taylor Lautner was setting a standard for ab-ulousness, a message the other wolf-pack actors took from the very start.

"Some of them were in extraordinary shape anyway," says producer Wyck Godfrey. "But the first day Taylor came on set, he pulls off his shirt and he's jacked. I mean humongous. And you kind of saw the look on all their faces. Some are sucking in their gut and sticking their chest out."

Bronson Pelletier readily admits he showed up biceps-strong but a little pudgy, thinking the most he'd be on-screen was sleeveless. Then he got on set for a photo shoot fitting and heard, "Okay, get undressed, here's a pair of shorts." Recalls Bronson, "I was like, 'Um, where's my shirt?' Then we were told we were getting personal trainers. I remember one of the wolf-pack guys made a joke. 'It's because of Bronson, isn't it?' And the assistant director said, 'Yeah.' I thought, 'Oh, my pride!'"

What followed was an intensive workout regimen of five to six days a week that might have broken the will of lesser actors: circuit training, strength training, elements of Brazilian jujitsu and muay thai boxing, exercises that involved swinging kettlebells, pull-ups on Olympic rings, and taking sledgehammers to 450-pound construction tires (when the guys weren't having to flip them over and run through them).

For Chaske Spencer, the transformation happened within weeks. "It was really weird to just go from being a toothpick to this mass of muscle in a matter of under a month."

The training served another purpose, too: It bonded the actors, strengthening their camaraderie so they could easily project a brotherhood of beefcake. Football proved to be another favorite wolf-pack pastime (even inside a cramped tent when it was raining).

Tinsel Korey remembers the testosterone displays. "They would compete doing curl-ups off the beam in Emily's house," she recalls, and adds laughingly, "I had the toughest job in the world. I got to hang around set all day and stare at half-naked men. Hey, good time!"

In their efforts to bulk up, the pack members were constantly eating, spending their daily cash allowances at Vancouver steakhouses like The Keg and Milestones. The result, though, was more than just a charismatic gang of ripped new movie studs, but a well-knit band, connected on-screen and off, a group of friends who've stayed in touch since wrapping up the saga and who may personify the telepathy Stephenie Meyer bestowed upon her werewolf creations. "To this day," Chaske says, "if you get us all in a room together, we pretty much can read each other's minds." ∎

(BELOW) The wolf pack on the set of *Breaking Dawn - Part 1*

Animator Phil Tippett, NEW MOON director Chris Weitz, and Alex Meraz rehearse wolf movements.

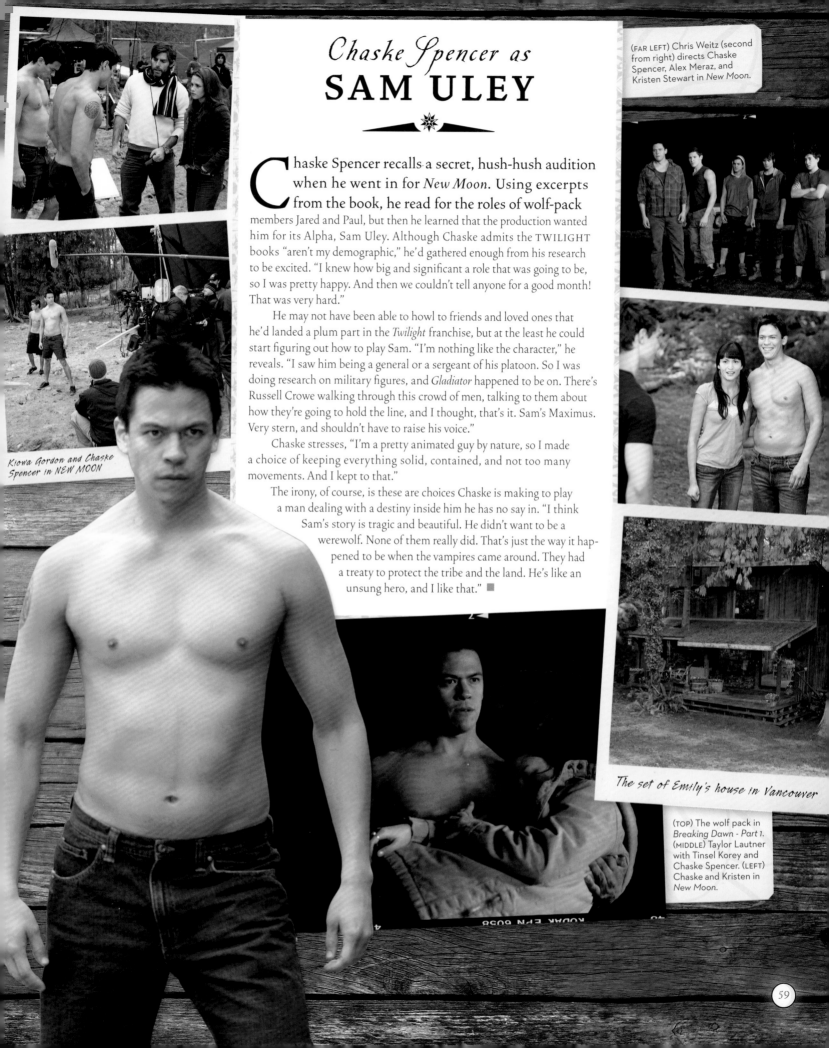

Chaske Spencer as
SAM ULEY

Chaske Spencer recalls a secret, hush-hush audition when he went in for *New Moon*. Using excerpts from the book, he read for the roles of wolf-pack members Jared and Paul, but then he learned that the production wanted him for its Alpha, Sam Uley. Although Chaske admits the TWILIGHT books "aren't my demographic," he'd gathered enough from his research to be excited. "I knew how big and significant a role that was going to be, so I was pretty happy. And then we couldn't tell anyone for a good month! That was very hard."

He may not have been able to howl to friends and loved ones that he'd landed a plum part in the *Twilight* franchise, but at the least he could start figuring out how to play Sam. "I'm nothing like the character," he reveals. "I saw him being a general or a sergeant of his platoon. So I was doing research on military figures, and *Gladiator* happened to be on. There's Russell Crowe walking through this crowd of men, talking to them about how they're going to hold the line, and I thought, that's it. Sam's Maximus. Very stern, and shouldn't have to raise his voice."

Chaske stresses, "I'm a pretty animated guy by nature, so I made a choice of keeping everything solid, contained, and not too many movements. And I kept to that."

The irony, of course, is these are choices Chaske is making to play a man dealing with a destiny inside him he has no say in. "I think Sam's story is tragic and beautiful. He didn't want to be a werewolf. None of them really did. That's just the way it happened to be when the vampires came around. They had a treaty to protect the tribe and the land. He's like an unsung hero, and I like that." ■

(FAR LEFT) Chris Weitz (second from right) directs Chaske Spencer, Alex Meraz, and Kristen Stewart in *New Moon*.

The set of Emily's house in Vancouver

(TOP) The wolf pack in *Breaking Dawn - Part 1*. (MIDDLE) Taylor Lautner with Tinsel Korey and Chaske Spencer. (LEFT) Chaske and Kristen in *New Moon*.

THE CULLEN HOUSE

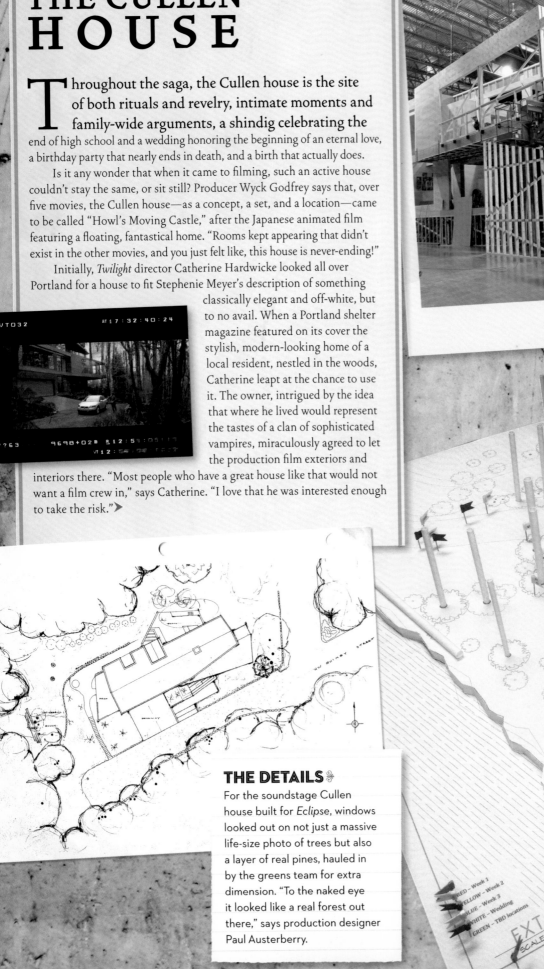

Throughout the saga, the Cullen house is the site of both rituals and revelry, intimate moments and family-wide arguments, a shindig celebrating the end of high school and a wedding honoring the beginning of an eternal love, a birthday party that nearly ends in death, and a birth that actually does.

Is it any wonder that when it came to filming, such an active house couldn't stay the same, or sit still? Producer Wyck Godfrey says that, over five movies, the Cullen house—as a concept, a set, and a location—came to be called "Howl's Moving Castle," after the Japanese animated film featuring a floating, fantastical home. "Rooms kept appearing that didn't exist in the other movies, and you just felt like, this house is never-ending!"

Initially, *Twilight* director Catherine Hardwicke looked all over Portland for a house to fit Stephenie Meyer's description of something classically elegant and off-white, but to no avail. When a Portland shelter magazine featured on its cover the stylish, modern-looking home of a local resident, nestled in the woods, Catherine leapt at the chance to use it. The owner, intrigued by the idea that where he lived would represent the tastes of a clan of sophisticated vampires, miraculously agreed to let the production film exteriors and interiors there. "Most people who have a great house like that would not want a film crew in," says Catherine. "I love that he was interested enough to take the risk." ▸

THE DETAILS ❧

For the soundstage Cullen house built for *Eclipse*, windows looked out on not just a massive life-size photo of trees but also a layer of real pines, hauled in by the greens team for extra dimension. "To the naked eye it looked like a real forest out there," says production designer Paul Austerberry.

➤ What came to be known as such a distinctive set was only a location-filming source for *Twilight*, however. With *New Moon* shooting in Vancouver as opposed to Portland, and only one big scene—Bella's birthday party—taking place at the Cullen house, the production opted to film inside an architecturally similar residence in Vancouver instead, using existing exterior shots of the original house as needed. "We were never in the same rooms that we'd used in *Twilight*, so it all worked out," says Wyck.

Eclipse was a different situation. With so many scenes taking place at the house, rebuilding proved essential. *Eclipse* production designer Paul Austerberry secured rights to the Portland house's plans from the original architects, Skylab Architecture, and erected a replica inside the 20,000-square-foot Vancouver soundstage. Judicious "cheating" meant that only two of the three stories were built, with top-floor interiors re-created on the second using moveable walls and creative re-dressing. (Edward's bedroom in *Eclipse* is actually the living room transformed.)

By the time of *Breaking Dawn*, for which Cullen house scenes fairly dominate, the filming had been moved to Louisiana. But when no site could be found that offered realistic Pacific Northwest–style vegetation and a river, Vancouver was called upon for service once more. This meant *two* Cullen houses: a rebuilding of the *Eclipse* house on a Baton Rouge soundstage, and a two-story location in secluded Squamish, British Columbia. New spaces being seen for the first time included Carlisle's first-floor study, Alice's top-floor bedroom, and the entire back of the house overlooking the site of the wedding.

Splitting up the house duties between a soundstage set and a secluded outdoor location, however, paid enormous dividends in terms of on-screen reality, says Wyck. "I think we finally captured the locale Stephenie envisioned—that they lived right by a river, that the house was in the middle of the woods where you really felt like nobody would ever come around."

For *Breaking Dawn* director Bill Condon, the experience of shooting on two identical sets thousands of miles apart led to what he describes as "one of the most magical experiences" he's ever had on a movie. For seven months in Baton Rouge, Bill had only known the interior set and the massive greenscreen around it. "The staircase, Carlisle's study, these spaces have become your working environment, and you know every nook and cranny so well. And then you arrive in Vancouver, you go to the set, and it's exactly this thing you've known so intimately, except now you look outside and there's this spectacular world out there. It was unbelievably weird to have a house that exists in two places."

Bill then adds, "The punch line of this is, vampires may stay the same, but their houses morph and change in mysterious ways." ∎

On the set of ECLIPSE, getting the Cullen house ready for filming the nighttime graduation party

Elizabeth Reaser as
ESME CULLEN

For Elizabeth Reaser, it was the image of a nurturing vampire mom playing hostess to her son's human girlfriend that drew the actress to *Twilight.* "That scene in particular—at the time I thought it was really fascinating," says Elizabeth. "Just how strange those vampires were to me at the time, that they're vegetarians, excited about this new person coming into their world, but for purer reasons. Not because we want to eat her!"

Esme Cullen is incapable of seeing bad in people, explains Elizabeth. "She's just so loving, and I think that's her real gift. In the lore, when you're a human, whatever's a strong quality in you becomes super-exaggerated as a vampire, so her ability to love became extra and maternal. For her, everybody is the best person they can possibly be. I mean, she even loves the werewolves!"

But outside Esme's warm looks and offers of food, Elizabeth loved that she got to assert herself in *Breaking Dawn - Part 1* when danger was at the Cullens' door. "It made sense to me, considering the women and mothers I've known in my life. They're not the person in the family that takes a backseat. It seemed believable to me that mama bear—if she loves to that degree— would come out and take a real stance."

Although she's heard her fair share of "I wish you were my mom!" from fans, she especially treasures the positive responses to the romance between Esme and Carlisle Cullen, since Elizabeth adores her on-screen husband, Peter Facinelli. "When you do five movies with someone, you get to know them in a way that no other situation provides. He's someone I really care about, and just a joy to run into at four in the morning in the hair and makeup trailer, or to stand with in the freezing rain as you wait to run through a forest. He was always cool and funny and would crack me up." ■

On the set of ECLIPSE

Filming the showdown in BREAKING DAWN - PART 2

Xavier Samuel and Robert Pattinson filming a scene in ECLIPSE

"I got a nice copy of BREAKING DAWN, a hardcover, and got everyone to sign it. You draw a fine line when you're working with such huge megastars—if you ask them, even as a castmate, for their autograph in a book, are you diminishing yourself in some way? So I jokingly said to Kristen, 'Kristen, will you sign my yearbook?' And she was really lovely. So when she was signing it, she wrote something like, 'Toni, it's been so fun! Have a great summer!' Something you would see in a yearbook. Those things are really invaluable, I think." —Toni Trucks (Mary)

"We were filming in this artificial snowy studio landscape, and I took a little twig, but I gave it to a friend of mine who was quite a fan of the films, so she's got a little twig on her desk. I wonder how much that would go for on eBay." —Xavier Samuel (Riley)

"When I was in Baton Rouge, I had a four-day sojourn into New Orleans, and I was in this antiques store, because I collect silver napkin rings. Well, I found one and it was engraved 'Renée,' and I thought that was so cool. I was like, 'And I have to buy that!'"
—Sarah Clarke (Renée)

"My souvenir was my love of Vancouver. I'm gonna have my baby here, because my husband's working here. And I'm actually in the same building that I stayed in when I was shooting *Eclipse*. I just loved everything about the experience."
—Bryce Dallas Howard (Victoria)

"I have Carlisle's ring. Unless they ask for it back, and then I don't have Carlisle's ring." —Peter Facinelli (Carlisle)

"I didn't realize we were allowed to take souvenirs! Apparently I'm the only person who didn't take a souvenir from set. I know people took stuff, but Emily is true to her pack, and I'm gonna stay true to that and not say anything." —Tinsel Korey (Emily)

"Oh boy. Um . . . we may or may not have taken some . . . silverware from the wedding. Several people were involved. Or may or may not have been involved." —Casey LaBow (Kate)

"On set they have chairs for the actors, and it has your name on the back. I have all of my seat backs, so I kept those. Those are cool. I have them hanging up on the wall of my apartment." —Chaske Spencer (Sam)

"I have these great little gloves. They're just kind of brown, little fingerless gloves, that very old but new vamp look that did so well with the Romanians. I was like, 'I need something, come on! I can't walk away with nothing!' Don't tell anybody!" —Noel Fisher (Vladimir)

"I'm gonna be in so much trouble for this. I didn't have a warm coat when we came to Louisiana, because I thought, well, I'm in the Deep South, it's not gonna be cold! I was very wrong, and being foolish and not American, I was incredibly wrong, and it was freezing. We had bouts of snow, even, and hail. So I had a warming coat on set between scenes, which was the toastiest, most wonderful, most fantastic thing I've ever worn ever in my life, so I'm currently wearing it. I'm sorry, Michael Wilkinson, but yeah, I've got your warming coat."
—MyAnna Buring (Tanya)

the twilight saga
new moon

Ashley Greene as
ALICE CULLEN

W hen Ashley Greene first read the TWILIGHT books, the character of Alice drew her in immediately. "There were so many qualities I could relate to: her fierce dedication to her family, her glass-half-full attitude, and her sweet demeanor," says the actress, whose lively persona on-screen has made her a fan favorite when it comes to Cullen clan portrayals.

Ashley thinks the fandom responds to Alice because "she's a positive, optimistic force that can't help but make you smile. She's loving, loyal, and a bit sassy. You can't help but feel like she is your best friend."

When it came to getting the part, however, Ashley admits she told a "little fib" concerning her athletic abilities. "I said I knew how to pitch, and I really had no idea how to throw a baseball!" she reveals about her prospects on the mound for the baseball scene in *Twilight*. "Luckily, I had a lot of boys around me who helped me out, and a pro pitcher. Then I just left it to the movie gods, and somehow everything came together."

Producer Wyck Godfrey adds his observations regarding Ashley's dedication: "If you had seen what she looked like two weeks into rehearsal, out by the soundstages throwing that baseball, you would have been like 'Oh my God, we're doomed.' And then, by the time we shot that scene, she gets her leg kick up and really guns it in there, and it ended up looking really great. I think it's kind of a cool little thing that she took on." Now Ashley has had to deal with letting go of Alice, and it hasn't been easy. "I'd lived with her for four years," she says. "She became a big part of my life, so saying goodbye is hard. I'll never forget the experiences I've had." ■

They turn as Alice skips into the room, the others follow, lining up to present Bella with something.

EDWARD
(gently to Bella)
Let Rosalie take her for a while.

Bella can sense something's up as Rosalie scoops Renesmee out of her reluctant arms.

Finally Alice extends her hand - in it lies a KEY with a ribbon tied to it.

ALICE
Happy Birthday!

Off Bella, confused, apprehensive -- *birthday?* --

EXT. FOREST - NIGHT

CLOSE ON BELLA'S FACE - ALICE'S HANDS ARE OVER HER EYES as she's blindly guided up a path.

BELLA
No -- I stopped aging three days ago!

ALICE (O.S.)
We're celebrating anyway, so suck it up.

BELLA
I hate surprises, *that* hasn't changed --

ALICE (O.S.)
You'll love this one.

Suddenly, Alice pulls her hands away - Bella takes in what's in front of her, is stunned, as we REVEAL --

A BEAUTIFUL STONE COTTAGE

Honeysuckle climbs up its side to thick wooden shingles. Roses bloom under deep-set windows. A path of flat stones leads to a wooden door.

ALICE
Welcome home!

Bella is speechless. Alice and Edward aren't sure what to make of her reaction.

Ashley Greene and E. J. Foerster on the set of ECLIPSE

▤ PRODUCER'S TAKE

"She was just born to play Alice. She just has that pixie quality, where you'll be having a conversation with her, and then, boom, the camera goes on, and her voice changes a tone. She goes a little bit more to that flighty, singsongy voice that's really representative of Alice's bubbly personality." —Wyck Godfrey

(FROM LEFT) Drawing of Rosalie's pendant, Edward's leather cuff, Cullen crest pendants. (BELOW) Volturi crest.

THE DETAILS

In one of the designs for the Volturi crest, Rick Thurber of Artisan's Designs incorporated a single pearl, three diamonds in a V shape, and a circle of small teeth surrounding an Italian tower. Petrified dinosaur bone had also been requested. "Thankfully, I found a guy in Wisconsin with a slab of it!" says Rick. In the end, another design was ultimately used for the Volturi crest, but this particular one was repurposed for the Volturi throne backs.

THE JEWELRY
OF *TWILIGHT*

One of the biggest changes the *Twilight* movies made in adapting Stephenie Meyer's books was an addition: giving the Cullens a regal, intricate family crest that they continuously wear emblazoned on jewelry. Inspired by an idea from *Twilight* costume designer Wendy Chuck, and designed by director Catherine Hardwicke and her team, the crest gave the Cullens a unifying symbol of strength (the lion), sincerity (the hand), and perpetuity (the band of trefoils) to which fans immediately responded with enthusiasm.

Artisan's Designs, of Portland, Oregon, was called into action to make the sterling-silver pieces worn by the Cullens: Alice's velvet-ribboned choker, Rosalie's pendant, Esme's bracelet, Carlisle's ring, and the leather wristbands seen on Edward, Emmett, and Jasper. Duplicates were also made for stunt doubles. In all, Rick Thurber of Artisan's estimates he's made more than a hundred pieces for *Twilight*, *New Moon*, and *Eclipse*, including Bella's moonstone ring, and her engagement ring for *Eclipse*.

Artisan's wasn't used for *The Twilight Saga: Breaking Dawn*, though. Besides the fact that there were enough pieces already, the decision was made that the Cullens didn't need to be wearing the crest all the time, and when it came to making new pieces, costume designer Michael Wilkinson stepped in for a fashion-forward take on some of the jewelry. "We reappropriated the crest from Alice's high velvet choker and made a multistrand, low-hanging piece that we felt was more contemporary. And similarly for Rosalie, we put her crest on a beautiful chain, and we decided to make it higher, so it sits beautifully on the collarbone."

Michael is also proud of the pieces he created for the Denali sisters for *Breaking Dawn - Part 2*, which incorporate symbols that show not only the influence of the Alaskan region they live in, but also the Russia of their family's origins. "We put the essence of both together into necklaces that reflect their own kind of boho chic aesthetic," says Michael. "And we worked

A close-up of Bella's engagement ring, first shown in ECLIPSE

(TOP TO BOTTOM) Alice's choker, Carlisle's ring, Cullen crest bracelet, wolf carved by Jacob. (LEFT) Sketch of Bella's engagement ring.

with a designer named Erin Wasson, who has a jewelry company called Low Luv. She helped us out with some beautiful rings and earrings for the three Denali sisters." Wasson's modern-yet-primitive aesthetic worked perfectly with Michael's take on the Denalis' tastes. "We thought the Denalis, who have been around for many centuries, would appreciate things that had this sort of older feel to them."

Since the first movie came out, crest items have become incredibly popular. (Even with the actors! Peter Facinelli tried to take Carlisle's ring with him after *New Moon* but had to bring it back for reshoots, while Ashley Greene simply held on to Alice's first necklace after the saga completed filming.) Fans have purchased pieces from individual makers who've created their own jewelry inspired by the Cullens' crest, and replicas from licensed sellers such as Artisan's Designs. Rick says he's sold Cullen jewelry to far-flung countries from Italy to Australia. The crest's popularity has also inspired fans to imagine what their own family-related jewelry might look like. "I've had people from around the country take the frilly design around it and use their own crest in the middle to make their own pieces," says Rick.

Ultimately, the crest has proved as iconic for the movies as the Batman logo or the mockingjay emblem from *The Hunger Games*. As Summit executive Gillian Bohrer points out, "There are T-shirts that don't say anything about *Twilight*, that just have the image of the crest. It's an identifying symbol of the series without even needing to reference the name." ■

Peter Facinelli as
CARLISLE CULLEN

From the minute Peter Facinelli's Dr. Carlisle Cullen glides into the hospital wing with reassuring words for a shaken-up (but puzzled) Bella, it was clear that Stephenie Meyer's creation was going to be a different take on the vampire: friendly, calming, unfazed by wounded humans, and ready to help. "People always ask me when I started doing *Twilight* if I did a lot of research on being a vampire," says Peter, "and I say no, because Carlisle is kind of an antivampire. He never really embraced it, so for me it was more a study on humanity, why he wanted to retain his human traits, and what human traits he held on to."

As for Carlisle's special power—compassion—Peter cracks, "That's not really helpful in battle: You can't smite people with your compassion." But he recognizes a personal power in the doctor's long-standing effort to reject vampires' nomadic, brutal lifestyle. "That compassion comes out of his love for humanity, and I think there is a strength there."

With Carlisle more than 350 years old—and at the time of filming *Twilight*, with no Meyer-penned illustrated guide for easy backstory reference—Peter initially helped himself get into character by creating a history journal of places and events at which Carlisle might have been present. "I kind of built him from the ground up. It was like a big history lesson for me, and I thought, if I mapped out his whole three hundred fifty years, then somehow that would just live on-screen." ➤

Animal blood reserves for a pregnant Bella—just what the doctor ordered!

It led to one of the actor's proudest contributions, during the baseball sequence, when Carlisle re-creates Babe Ruth's called shot at the 1932 World Series, in which the legendary ballplayer pointed the bat to where he subsequently swatted a homer. Says Peter, "One thing I wrote was, why did Carlisle enjoy baseball so much? I thought maybe he had been at that game. So I went to Catherine Hardwicke and said, 'It'd be really fun if that's his thing; he always points his bat at center field and tries to hit it there,' and Esme would be like, 'Not the Babe Ruth thing again.' So we did it, and it's in the movie. That's the fun part of creating a character, those little tidbits you come up with that nobody will ever know what they meant, but they're meaningful for you as a character."

Carlisle's penchant for scarves, something not in the books, was Peter's idea as well. Initially the idea was that Carlisle's neckwear—something adopted in previous centuries—was a security blanket for him, a way to keep more of him from being exposed than necessary. For *Eclipse*, though, Peter found a way to retire the scarves for the newborn battle. "When the wolves come down to join us to train, I remove my scarf when I thank them for helping us, and to my mind it was Carlisle showing vulnerability to get their respect and loyalty," says Peter. "From that scene on, I never wore it. That much thought goes behind things like that for me." ■

Peter Facinelli filming an action moment for BREAKING DAWN - PART 2

"Alice can see into the future a bit, which is pretty cool, although I suppose it would kind of ruin things a little bit. Jane's [power] is pretty sadistic. 'I just want this person to feel a little bit of pain, a twinge . . . a little bit of discomfort.' Speed is pretty cool. I'd take that. Save time. Getting around a bit quicker." —Xavier Samuel (Riley)

"Honestly, I really do love the idea of Jasper's power, the ability to influence emotion. I believe very fervently that the artist's job is to be able to influence emotion; whether you're a painter or a photographer or an actor or a musician, your job is to influence someone to feel something. It's not your job to tell them exactly what to feel, but it's your job to hopefully influence them to a certain degree to be open to emotion, whether that emotion is love or sadness or happiness or anger. Your job as an artist is to create emotion. So I think that's really what I've always been attuned to with Jasper." —Jackson Rathbone (Jasper)

"Their movement. Their ability to sort of jump and run and climb up those trees at that speed. Come on, wouldn't that be incredible? I'd be on a permanent holiday if I could do that. I'd just be running around the world scaling massive trees and jumping across oceans. It'd be incredible." —MyAnna Buring (Tanya)

"In reality? Probably the mind reading. I totally would love to have the mind reading. I'm such a detective by nature. I think it would really help me answer a lot of questions that I'm constantly asking myself, or of other people." —Casey LaBow (Kate)

"I love Alice's power with the vision, even though with Alice, she sometimes can't trust those visions. I think it would be so great, without even moving, to be able to just cause someone pain. Jane is cool as a cucumber, and she'll just ever so quietly whisper 'Pain' and people drop to the floor. I'm like, 'That is the best superpower ever!' Of course, I always say my Toni Trucks superpower would just be to turn things into ice cream. Or say 'Chocolate' and then your car would just be made out of Hershey's Kisses." —Toni Trucks (Mary)

"In real life? I'd like to fly. I'm sick and tired of hopping on planes. I wouldn't mind just hopping up in the sky and going for it." —Daniel Cudmore (Felix)

THE HOUSE OF VOLTURI

They make their first entrance amid the turbulent adventures of NEW MOON, this cloaked, authoritatively menacing coven of art-loving, Italy-based vampires known as the Volturi. Ancient enforcers of undead law, their protective view of the way the vampire world works—live secretly, hunt humans judiciously, create newborns responsibly—has led them to serious clashes with exposure-threatening covens around the world.

So when the Cullens bring human Bella Swan into their family, it ignites a handful of problems that the Volturi mean to address quickly—through punitive exercises of pure power. Thousands of years of de facto rule, after all, might make anyone overreact to a threat to tradition. *New Moon* director Chris Weitz jokingly describes the Volturi as characters who "have been around so long that they've gone kind of nuts."

As the villains of Stephenie Meyer's mythology, however, their actions provide plenty of the saga's tension: Volturi guard member Felix's marble-shattering fight with Edward Cullen in *New Moon*; innocent-looking Jane's ability to bring a world of hurt to someone by simply saying "Pain"; and in *Breaking Dawn - Part 2*, a massive show of Volturi force in response to fears about Edward and Bella's child, Renesmee. Although fans have generally been excited at running into the actors who play the Volturi, there are the occasional dirty looks toward those who represent the stories' deadliest obstacle to Bella-Edward happiness.

Says Cameron Bright, who plays paralysis-wielding twin brother Alec to Dakota Fanning's Jane, "At the end of the day everybody knows it's a movie. But it's funny— I get scowled at every once in a while. I laugh at it. Hey, it's my job to be a bad guy, so I don't mind!" ■

The Volturi thrones for Marcus, Aro, and Caius on the set of NEW MOON

Michael Sheen as
ARO

With Aro, Welsh actor Michael Sheen saw an opportunity to get under moviegoers' skin the way classic villains from films of his youth did, such as the child catcher in *Chitty Chitty Bang Bang* or the Blue Meanies from *Yellow Submarine*. Stephenie Meyer described Aro as having a voice like feathers. "I got the sense of a character who played at being a kindly, sentimental romantic—an old grandmother, almost," says Michael, "and yet underneath was a heartless killer."

He chalks up a certain measure of Aro's pathology to the drawbacks of underground-lair life away from human contact. "You'd start to go a little bit crazy, cabin feverish. Or lair feverish. The boredom factor would probably be the hardest thing about eternal life, so when anything new comes along—like this young love between Bella and Edward—then you can see how it becomes exciting."

When he was initially in talks for the role, Sheen went straight to his daughter, Lily, a fan of the books. "It's one of the great powers of what Stephenie has written," he says, "that it speaks especially to younger girls identifying with Bella's journey."

The Welsh actor has considered his *Twilight* role "a real adventure and a real joy," from getting to know the cast and crew to talking about books with Stephenie and relishing the impact the stories have on young people. "Usually I'm working with old fuddy-duddies," he says. "So getting to work with these vibrant young people is wonderful. Although it does make you feel very old and ugly standing around them!"

Even Lily got onboard. "In her bedroom she had posters up of Bella and different *Twilight* characters, along with other things like the Beatles, but one day I came into her bedroom and saw in the corner, among all these pictures, a small cutout of me from a magazine. And I thought that was a very proud moment." ∎

Michael Sheen and NEW MOON director Chris Weitz

A Volturi bloodbath, in a scene deleted from BREAKING DAWN - PART 1

(CLOCKWISE FROM TOP LEFT)
Charlie Bewley, Cameron Bright, Dakota Fanning, and Daniel Cudmore in *Eclipse*; Cameron as Alec; Daniel (Felix) grabbing Jodelle Ferland (Bree Tanner) in *Eclipse*; Charlie as Demetri

Jane turns to Bella but Edward springs in front of her --
ready to attack. So Jane instead focuses her gaze on
Edward. She looks at him dispassionately, completely
unafraid of him. Edward moves towards him, then, at a word
from Jane --

                    JANE
                    Pain.

He freezes. For a second he holds his position, his face
twisted with strain. Then he crumples under the pain of her
gaze. He can no longer fight the pain. He writhes on the
stones at Jane's feet. Jane smiles.

                    BELLA
                    Stop it!

She is about to run towards Jane but Alec is there, standing
in her way, smiling and slowly wagging his finger -- a
badidea. In his other hand he has her wrist in an iron grip.

                    BELLA
Stop it! Please! Stop hurting him! Do what you have to do to
me!

As soon as Jane looks away, Edward's pain ceases. Alec lets
go of Bella. She and Bella look at each other now. Bella,
defiant. Alice rushes to Edward's side.

                    ARO
                    Go ahead, Jane.

                    JANE
                    (smiles; to Bella)
          This may hurt just a little.

Jane concentrates... Bella cringes, awaiting the pain... but
nothing happens. Jane's grin is replaced by anger. Aro laughs
like a child with a new toy.

Jane stalks towards Bella; Aro stops her with a gesture.

Dakota Fanning as
JANE

With Volturi member Jane, one word can start the hurting (and it isn't even real—you're just imagining it), but for Dakota Fanning, getting to play that kind of casual evil for *The Twilight Saga* was a career high.

"I was really excited to get to play one of the villains in the story, since I've never really done that in my life before," says the former child star.

New Moon director Chris Weitz calls Dakota "not only one of these young actresses who is kind of sophisticated in terms of technique beyond her years but is also just a lovely, lovely person."

When she was tapped to join the Volturi coven, she embraced the mixture of surface youth and centuries-old experience that made Jane one of the more striking vampires in Stephenie Meyer's gallery of red-eyed rogues. Says Dakota, "She's lived over a thousand years yet still looks like a young girl, and I think she takes advantage of this weird innocence she has and that Aro sees in her. It makes her even creepier. You might not realize what she's capable of at first."

It quickly becomes apparent in *New Moon*, though. Dakota laughs at the memory of fretting over what it would mean for her acceptance by the fandom. "I was afraid I wasn't going to have any fans, because I do 'pain' Rob! I was like, 'Oh no, they're going to hate me!'"

Instead, there have been plenty of excited moviegoers who tell her how effectively scary and creepy she is in the saga. But the actress is never exactly sure if she's supposed to be appreciative or apologetic. "I say 'Thanks,' but then I feel weird saying thanks, because it's like, 'Sorry I was a weirdo in the movie and scared you, but that is what I was supposed to do!'"

Her friends have kidded her about her character's "get ready for pain" expression, which makes another appearance in *Breaking Dawn - Part 2*. "When the movies came out, they were like, 'I've seen that look before.' But I actually have a shirt with my face on it and Jane's line, 'This might hurt just a little.' I would just whip it out and say, 'Yeah, you don't want to see this.'" ∎

Getting a light reading

Dakota Fanning in her Jane getup, holding a copy of NEW MOON

On the set of *Breaking Dawn - Part 2*

FAN BITES:
UNDER THE TUSCAN *MOON*

I f the throngs attending the 2008 San Diego Comic-Con were one indication of how big the movie versions of TWILIGHT would become, the Italy shoot for *New Moon* was another. Like a global invasion, fans from around the world descended on the picturesque Tuscan city of Montepulciano in May of 2009 for a glimpse of Bella in a mad dash through packed streets and across a fountain to save a shirtless Edward from fatal daytime exposure.

The idea was fan friendly in the first place: Contests were held in dozens of countries to randomly select entrants for a trip to the set. But the production didn't take into consideration that all a committed Twilight fan needs—whether they've won a contest or not—is knowledge of where Kristen Stewart and Rob Pattinson will be on a given day for filming.

"All the people who submitted entries, they came anyway," recalls co-producer Bill Bannerman. "The contest had announced exactly when and where we'd be, so we couldn't go into hiding. That's why around five thousand people showed up out of nowhere three, four days before we arrived. Fans, their mothers, relatives, and the media, of course. But mostly fans."

The tourist explosion was difficult initially. "Our fans were so thick in those small streets that go from one side of town, where our art department was building our fountain set, to where our production office was that we just didn't bother at times. It was faster for us to jump on YouTube and watch fan downloads of what was going on blocks away than to actually walk the distance. Because the uploads were almost instantaneous, we were watching it within minutes of it happening." ➤

Red-cloaked extras in the streets of Montepulciano, subbing for Volterra

Overhead shot of the piazza where the Italy climax was filmed

ACTOR
CHARLIE BEWLEY
WRITES . . .

LOCATION: A small village that sits atop some desultory mound in the spectacular Tuscan wine-growing middle Italy. Nine centuries old is this little rustic dwelling, and looks it—not a hint of a commercial footprint, everything completely as it was all those years ago, complete with cobblestone streets, ghostly underground passageways, and small nook shops dealing in traditional products such as wine, biscotti, wine, olive oil, wine, Pinocchio puppets, and wine.

Journeying to the village for the first time, ascending the cutbacks and tight lanes, I felt my hairs begin to rise in building anticipation. It became quite apparent that a very special effort was being made to make the most of this special occasion.

The fans of Twilight had also arrived, breathing life into this *underworld*. They came in droves from far and wide—and who was going to stop them? This was a show as much as a job: Great work on the part of *The Twilight Saga*'s production and distribution company, Summit Entertainment, causing a second earthquake in the region in a matter of weeks.

In spite of a mozzarella hangover, waking up in the morning wasn't a problem; it was a pleasure. I wasn't alone in this sentiment. "When we wrapped, I stood in the street and cried," Rocco Gismondi (first assistant director, Italy) told me at the Last Supper of Relais San Bruno, our glorious hillside candlelit after-hours retreat. What I heard in Rocco's voice clarified my sentiments entirely: *Life may not get better than this.*

Chris Weitz (middle left) directing Kristen Stewart for the Italy sequence in NEW MOON

➤ Besides Rob and Kristen, the actors called for Italy duty were Daniel Cudmore and Charlie Bewley, who play Volturi guard members Felix and Demetri, and Dakota Fanning as Jane. They were filmed escorting Kristen through Volterra passageways. Daniel remembers the strange dichotomy of being in a medieval city emblematic of old-world charm and leisurely pleasures, yet lined with screaming fans there for a modern phenomenon. "You're in these old tunnels and wine cellars with cobwebs, mortared brick falling apart, and it's really neat. To be able to do that as an actor, you just pinch yourself. But then you're also pulling up in vans where people are banging on the windows thinking you might be Rob Pattinson or one of the Cullens. With that experience in that small fishbowl that was Italy, I really got a view of what the grand scope of this was all about."

The fans lined the narrow cobblestone streets, packed doorways, and crowded against barriers, while a select group of lucky visitors were chosen to be red-cloaked extras, possibly to be shoved aside by Kristen as she made her beeline for the heavy wooden doors of the church of Santa Maria delle Grazie.

"We shot for four days, and each day there were more and more [people], and they were everywhere, but very helpful," says *New Moon* director Chris Weitz. "Very observant of what it takes to make a movie. Very quiet when it came to rolling film. But the moment you called 'Cut!' it was thousands of people applauding. Which just doesn't happen on a film set. It was really something. Like doing theater in the round."

Producer Wyck Godfrey described it as "a chorus of angelic cheering every time Rob stepped out. You couldn't help but smile and say, 'Oh God, we are in a heightened reality now.'"

Once again, the Internet exploded with posted images, this time of Kristen's courtyard sprint into Rob's arms, as fans spread the word on what the end of *New Moon* might look like. "There was no way to control all the footage," Wyck recalls. "By the time I woke up the next morning, I was getting calls from Los Angeles saying, 'What the…? The entire scene is online!' And yet, it was kind of great."

One enterprising person had even taken all the available fan-uploaded photos and video from filming the Bella-Edward reunion and cut it together as a movie scene, set to music. "It really felt like, if you'd put that in the movie, that it would be great, it was so emotional," says Wyck. "I remember almost being moved to tears."

The Tuscan adventure marked the end of principal photography on *New Moon*, and for the fortunate souls who made the trek—whether as actors, crew, or tourists—it proved an unforgettable experience. "It's the most beautiful country in the world," says Chris. "Especially after slogging through looking at what seemed like every single tree in British Columbia at night, to go from that to Montepulciano, to be in that ancient town square in the Italian sun, worrying whether we'd have enough extras but realizing that there were fans who would happily throw on a red cloak to be in this big scene, and then to retire to [a bed-and-breakfast] to have food prepared by the grandma there, was incontrovertibly the most fun." ■

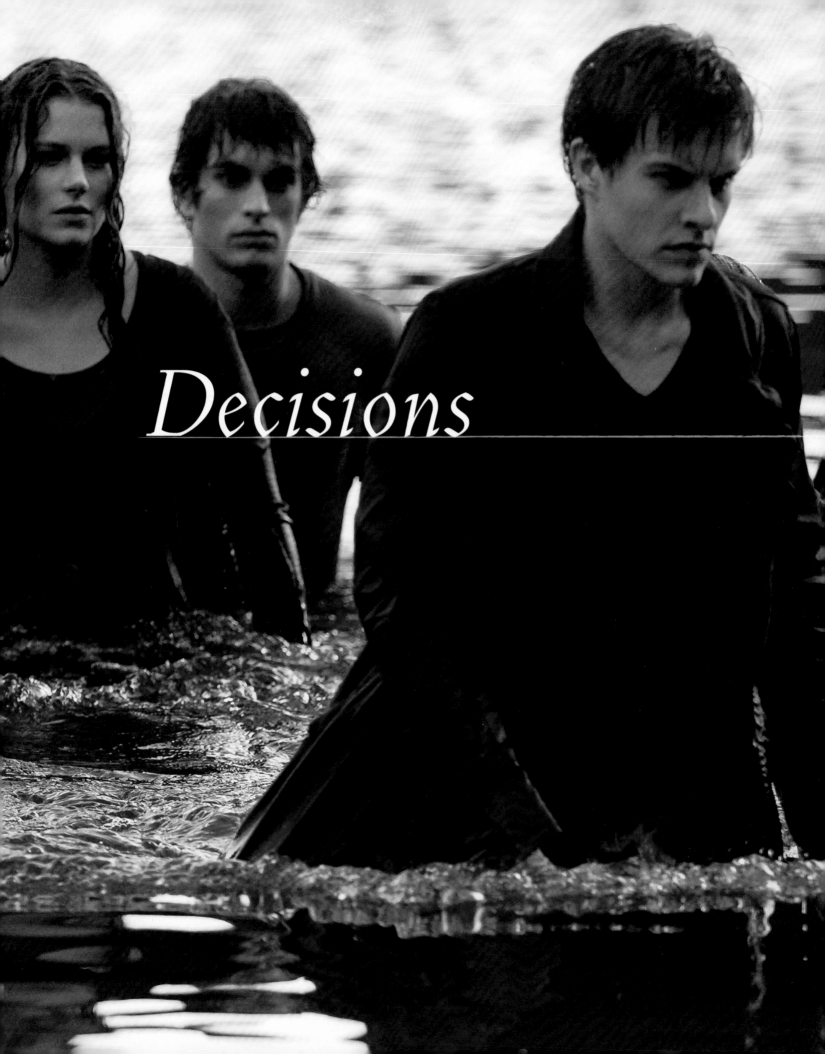

Decisions

(ABOVE RIGHT) David Slade directs Rob Pattinson and Kristen Stewart in *Eclipse*.

ECLIPSE director David Slade scopes out a sho[...]

Filming the emergence of the newborns from the water in ECLIPSE

DIRECTOR'S JOURNAL

DAVID SLADE TALKS *ECLIPSE*

Going into ECLIPSE, Summit understood they had a much darker book on their hands. Edward was once more in Bella's life, but now there were grim threats to explore as our heroine got comfortable with her choice to be with a vampire—namely, a burgeoning army of freshly turned vampires, manipulated by returning antagonist Victoria. The director of the acclaimed undead thriller *30 Days of Night*, David Slade, was the perfect choice to bring this book to the big screen.

In addition to capturing the darker side, David grasped what was central to the success of Stephenie Meyer's saga: the special connection between Bella and Edward. "One of the things that's so attractive about these stories and why they're successful is that they postulate the idea of true love in a world where it's not very common," David said in an interview during the making of *The Twilight Saga: Eclipse*. "To me, it's difficult to make a great story out of something as simple as pure love. Usually, great stories come from great conflicts. And what Stephenie's done so cleverly is made great conflict not at the expense of true love."

This movie was action-packed, too. Kellan Lutz, who plays Emmett Cullen, remembers a bit of direction David gave that helped him transform a physically tough moment into an emotionally useful one. "One of the hardest scenes was when my character fell into the water after a tumble with a wolf, and the water was really, really cold. But when you're a vampire you aren't supposed to get cold. David said to use the frigidness as anger. So when I'm huffing and puffing, it's not because I'm cold, but because I'm angry and want to fight this wolf." ➤

Grisly remains—what's left of the vanquished vampires from the *ECLIPSE* battle

The newborns, led by Riley (Xavier Samuel), making their move in *Eclipse*

"Part of the theme of *Eclipse* is the hunger of a newborn, the loss of control in becoming a vampire. I think the newborns represent the worst of what Bella can face," says producer Wyck Godfrey. "And I think David Slade, with his jagged, sharp-edged, uncomfortable style, is what we wanted to capture with *Eclipse*. That things aren't all cozy and wonderful now that Edward's back. Now there's something dark on the horizon. The Volturi are coming, the newborns are coming, there's going to be a battle."

The idea behind *Eclipse*, says Wyck, was to take Twilight fans into a whole different direction. Where *New Moon* had lingered in a kind of lush melancholy, *Eclipse* would aim for rawness, a visual discord that would match the same feeling Bella goes through in the movie. Plus, the third installment would ratchet up the excitement. "It had the most action, which David was really comfortable with, plus the darker elements of a vampire film," says Wyck. "For the first time you've got wolves biting the heads off vampires, and vampires crushing wolves."

Wyck says it's a testament to Stephenie's books and the movies that fans have stuck with what each new director brings to the table. "And that's partly because each time you're wondering, 'How are they going to handle the next one? What's it going to bring that we haven't seen before?'"

➤ "We did dump him in the river nine times," says David. "But he took it like a man, and every time he was up for more. He was a total hero about it."

The thrilling ravine chase with Victoria was a case of capturing something elemental about vampires—their foot speed—using real techniques rather than digital trickery. To that end, they rigged a "magic carpet" by which actors would run on a rug pulled by a truck going forty miles an hour, to simulate heightened speed. "I wanted it to be superhuman, not supernatural, because I believe that supernatural can be fantasy and divorce you from the screen," said David. "I wanted to ground the film in a space you would believe."

The most challenging day of shooting, according to David, was the one labeled Black Friday by the crew, because what should have been a fairly simple night shoot with Gil Birmingham as Billy Black giving some Quileute history around the campfire became a case of relentless rain. "Raindrops like marbles, the size of great big Californian cockroaches," jokes David. "And rain makes the noise of sizzling sausages. Gil Birmingham is giving the performance of his career, it's wonderful, and it sounds like sizzling sausages!"

Between the makeshift tarp covering the actors but always bulging with rainwater, the change in lighting so rain wouldn't show up on-screen, the shirtless wolf pack accidentally getting soaked, and reports of a bear sighting, it's a wonder the scene turned out as well as it did. Says David, "You would never know it was shot in the most horrific conditions."

Black Friday on the ECLIPSE set, when rain hampered a campfire scene

Much more idyllic to shoot—and appropriately so—were the meadow scenes that bookend the film. "We wanted to make it somewhat dreamlike at the beginning, to say, things are pretty perfect now, so perfect you could just float on air," described David, who chose to shoot through the flowers so that they could be a character in the scene, too. "They're interlinked with our protagonists. And when we return to the meadow again, we feel safe, we're in the same place, but these people have become more complicated." ∎

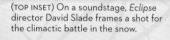

(TOP INSET) On a soundstage, *Eclipse* director David Slade frames a shot for the climactic battle in the snow.

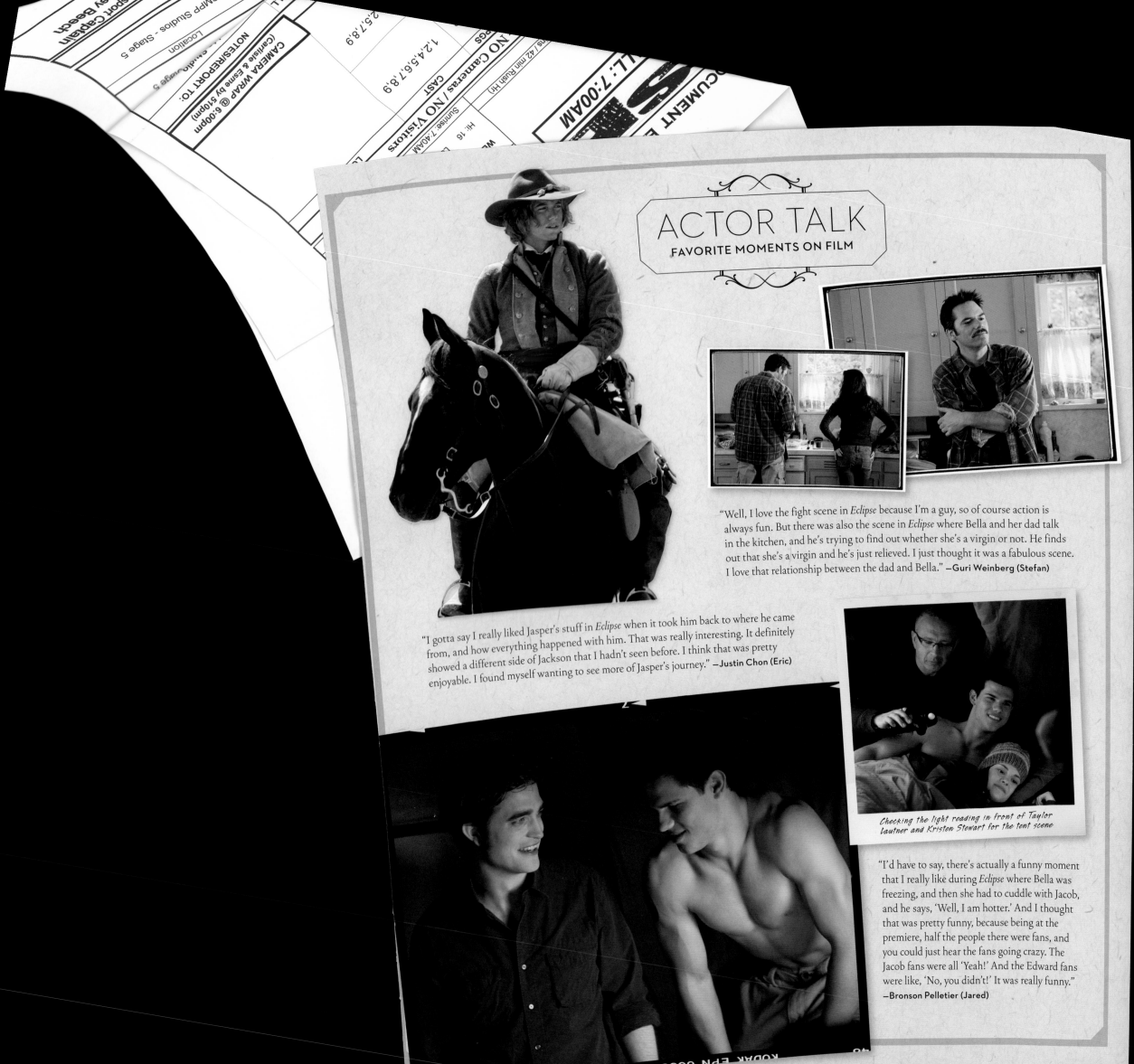

ACTOR TALK
FAVORITE MOMENTS ON FILM

"Well, I love the fight scene in *Eclipse* because I'm a guy, so of course action is always fun. But there was also the scene in *Eclipse* where Bella and her dad talk in the kitchen, and he's trying to find out whether she's a virgin or not. He finds out that she's a virgin and he's just relieved. I just thought it was a fabulous scene. I love that relationship between the dad and Bella." —Guri Weinberg (Stefan)

"I gotta say I really liked Jasper's stuff in *Eclipse* when it took him back to where he came from, and how everything happened with him. That was really interesting. It definitely showed a different side of Jackson that I hadn't seen before. I think that was pretty enjoyable. I found myself wanting to see more of Jasper's journey." —Justin Chon (Eric)

Checking the light reading in front of Taylor Lautner and Kristen Stewart for the tent scene

"I'd have to say, there's actually a funny moment that I really like during *Eclipse* where Bella was freezing, and then she had to cuddle with Jacob, and he says, 'Well, I am hotter.' And I thought that was pretty funny, because being at the premiere, half the people there were fans, and you could just hear the fans going crazy. The Jacob fans were all 'Yeah!' And the Edward fans were like, 'No, you didn't!' It was really funny." —Bronson Pelletier (Jared)

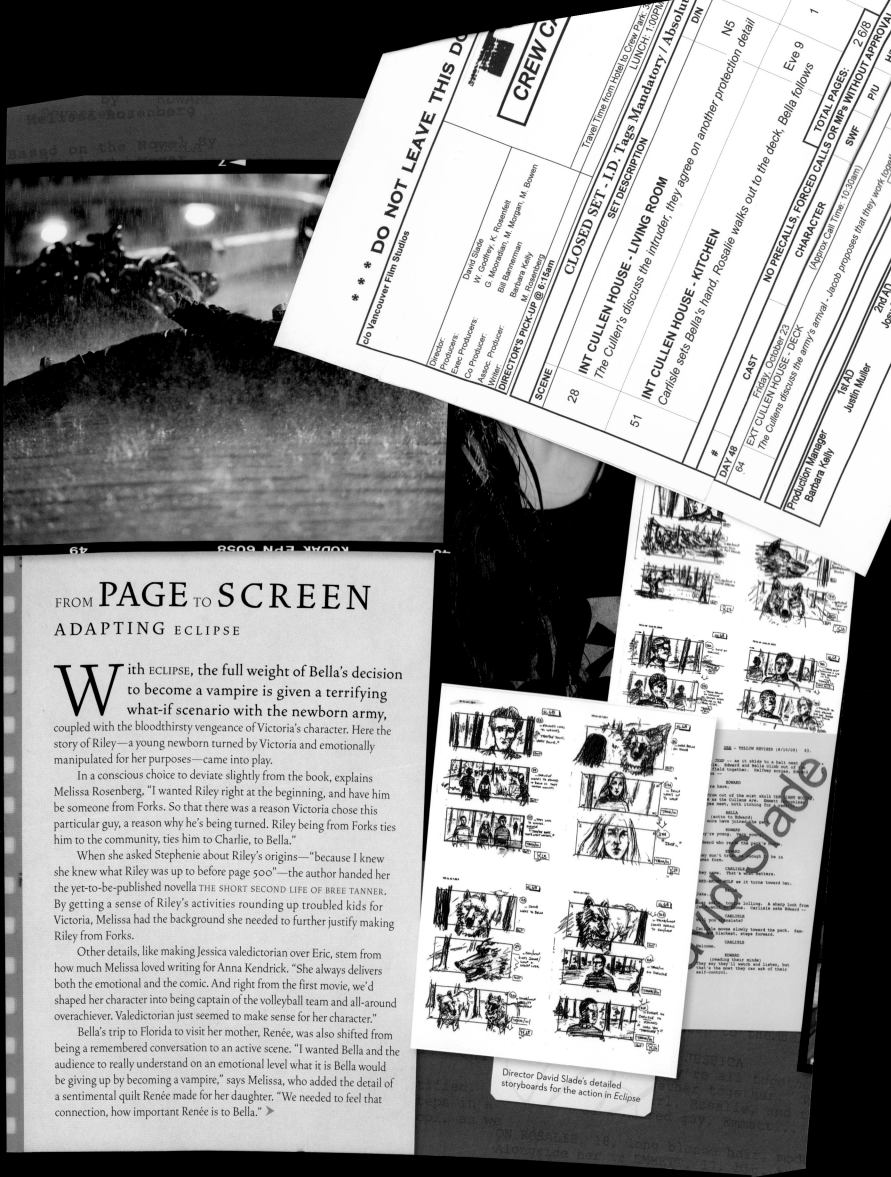

Director: David Slade
Producers: W. Godfrey, K. Rosenfelt
Exec Producers: G. Mooradian, M. Morgan, M. Bowen
Co Producer: Bill Bannerman
Assoc. Producer: Barbara Kelly
Writer: M. Rosenberg

DIRECTOR'S PICK-UP @ 6:15am

Travel Time from Hotel to Crew Park: 3[...]
LUNCH: 1:00PM[...] / Absolut[...]

CLOSED SET - I.D. Tags Mandatory / Absolut[...]

SCENE	SET DESCRIPTION	DIN[...]
28	**INT CULLEN HOUSE - LIVING ROOM** The Cullen's discuss the intruder, they agree on another protection detail	N5
51	**INT CULLEN HOUSE - KITCHEN** Carlisle sets Bella's hand, Rosalie walks out to the deck, Bella follows	Eve 9

#			TOTAL PAGES:	2 6/8
DAY 48	**NO PRECALLS, FORCED CALLS OR MPs WITHOUT APPROVAL O[...]**		MPs WITHOUT APPROVAL O[...]	

		CHARACTER	SWF	P/U	H/M/W	REHE[...]
64	EXT CULLEN HOUSE - DECK The Cullens discuss the army's arrival - Jacob proposes that they work together (Approx Call Time: 10:30am)			N10	3 2/8	1,2,3,4,...
	Friday, October 23			Total Pages:	3 2/8	

Production Manager: Barbara Kelly
1st AD: Justin Muller
2nd AD: Josy Capkun
Location Mgr: Abraham Fraser
ALM: Michael Legresley
On Set ALM: Dan Kuzmenko

FROM PAGE TO SCREEN
ADAPTING ECLIPSE

With ECLIPSE, the full weight of Bella's decision to become a vampire is given a terrifying what-if scenario with the newborn army, coupled with the bloodthirsty vengeance of Victoria's character. Here the story of Riley—a young newborn turned by Victoria and emotionally manipulated for her purposes—came into play.

In a conscious choice to deviate slightly from the book, explains Melissa Rosenberg, "I wanted Riley right at the beginning, and have him be someone from Forks. So that there was a reason Victoria chose this particular guy, a reason why he's being turned. Riley being from Forks ties him to the community, ties him to Charlie, to Bella."

When she asked Stephenie about Riley's origins—"because I knew she knew what Riley was up to before page 500"—the author handed her the yet-to-be-published novella THE SHORT SECOND LIFE OF BREE TANNER. By getting a sense of Riley's activities rounding up troubled kids for Victoria, Melissa had the background she needed to further justify making Riley from Forks.

Other details, like making Jessica valedictorian over Eric, stem from how much Melissa loved writing for Anna Kendrick. "She always delivers both the emotional and the comic. And right from the first movie, we'd shaped her character into being captain of the volleyball team and all-around overachiever. Valedictorian just seemed to make sense for her character."

Bella's trip to Florida to visit her mother, Renée, was also shifted from being a remembered conversation to an active scene. "I wanted Bella and the audience to really understand on an emotional level what it is Bella would be giving up by becoming a vampire," says Melissa, who added the detail of a sentimental quilt Renée made for her daughter. "We needed to feel that connection, how important Renée is to Bella." ➤

Director David Slade's detailed storyboards for the action in *Eclipse*

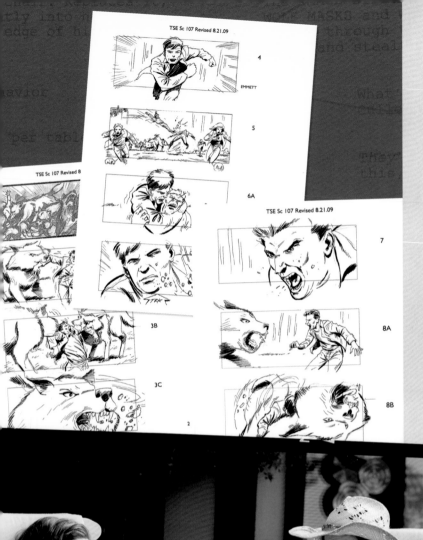

> Sometimes, though, a movie scene needs to be pretty much the way it is in the book, and that was the case with the chapter "Fire and Ice," which depicts a tense détente in the mountaintop cold where Jacob, keeping Bella warm, and Edward—who can only watch—hash out some differences between semifriendly verbal jabs. "It's Stephenie's favorite scene she ever wrote, so I wasn't going to screw that one up," says Melissa, laughing. "There was a lot more back-and-forth, so it was just what to pull out and where to condense. There was less invention. Except for Jacob's line 'I am hotter than you.' It's one of my favorite movie lines I ever wrote!"

The Twilight Saga: Eclipse had the most action of the *Twilight* movies to that point, but writing action in a screenplay isn't as clear-cut as describing each and every move. What's important, says Melissa, is indicating the story's intent when writing an action scene. "I may be specific enough to write, 'At this moment, Jacob-wolf lunges at . . .' and then name a particular vampire. That may not be exactly what happens, but the story is that Jacob is being heroic in this one moment. So maybe he doesn't lunge at that vampire, maybe he doesn't lunge at all, maybe he takes someone's head off. But the story is that Jacob is the hero."

With those story beats in mind, *Eclipse* director David Slade would then show Melissa detailed storyboards of how he saw the action choreography, maybe even acting out the various parts himself. Sometimes Melissa's action ideas were incorporated into the script. The object, though, was to get it all in the next draft of the script. "We went back and forth a lot until it was on the page, exactly what he wanted to shoot," says Melissa. "David's a very visual guy, very fun." ∎

Kristen Stewart and Sarah Clarke filming Bella's Florida visit with her mom, Renée, in *Eclipse*

85

Nikki Reed as
ROSALIE HALE

During the casting process for *Twilight*, Catherine Hardwicke showed her friend and *Thirteen* collaborator Nikki Reed the script. She wanted to know which female vampire character Nikki gravitated toward. No question, it was funny, rueful, and occasionally antagonistic Rosalie Hale.

After *Twilight* hit the screen, Nikki didn't always know how to deal with anti-Rosalie fans, but things started to change with the next several films. Rosalie's growing bond with Bella in *Eclipse* and *Breaking Dawn* helped to humanize the embittered vampire and brought out another side of her personality. "A major shift happened when I saw *Eclipse* with an audience," says Nikki. "I realized Rosalie's the comic relief."

This was especially evident while watching her flashback. Avenging her assault, she kills her fiancé while draped in snarling bridal white. The over-the-top scene was a crowd-pleaser, especially with the memorable line "I was a little theatrical back then." When Nikki heard the crowd laughing in the movie theater, she sensed a change in how people perceived her. There was understanding for her sadness, but also revelry in her flamboyance.

"She's just totally outrageous, and takes herself so seriously that you have to laugh when she's doing things like playing with her hair," says Nikki. After *Eclipse* she then went to *Breaking Dawn* director Bill Condon and asked for more comic moments for Rosalie. Although some scenes landed in the finished film, like the sight gag of her carrying an inhumanly heavy tree log in *Part 1*, other bits ended up on the cutting-room floor, like the Rosalie-Jacob dog-bowl fracas. Regardless, Nikki is grateful she hit upon this element of Rosalie during the process and had the revelation in a theater of Twilight fans. "That's been my journey with Rosalie, discovering that side of it, and I'm so happy I did." ■

THE DETAILS

When Catherine Hardwicke needed Nikki Reed to learn to bat with her opposite arm because of a camera setup, the pair's pre-*Twilight* friendship came into play. "She said, 'For you, I will learn this,'" recalls Catherine. "I was so proud of her. She really worked hard, and looked great doing it! Her slide into base, too! This was my third movie with Nikki, and it was really fun."

Nikki as Rosalie, in the ready position for the vampire-training scene in *Eclipse*

Design
Sketchbook

Producer Wyck Godfrey with a wedding gown–clad Nikki as Rosalie

Bryce Dallas Howard as
VICTORIA

Bryce Dallas Howard describes herself as "pretty levelheaded," but not about the saga of Bella and Edward. "I kind of lost it over TWILIGHT," the actress says, laughing. Her husband, actor Seth Gabel? Not so much. "When we found out that I was going to be doing *Eclipse*, he was genuinely like, 'I don't know what to think about this or how I feel about you spending time with Edward Cullen.' It's the only time in my professional career my husband was really concerned for me working with someone!"

(INSET) An early Catherine Hardwicke sketch for Victoria

Her enthusiasm, though, was tempered by the fact that she'd be taking over the role of Victoria from actress Rachelle Lefevre, who'd played the story's vengeful temptress in *Twilight* and *New Moon*, but who couldn't film *Eclipse* due to a scheduling conflict. "That was something I really kept in mind, honoring and acknowledging what Rachelle had brought to life. For audiences to say, 'Wait, why does Victoria suddenly seem really different?' would have undermined the storytelling."

Understanding the psychology of Victoria, who manipulates newborn Riley (Xavier Samuel) in her quest to get back at Edward for killing her soulmate James, was key for Bryce. "It's a fantasy, but imagine if your life lasts potentially a millennium, and the love of your life is murdered. You would go insane, because you're suddenly alone."

Though *Eclipse* and its bloodthirsty newborns are often seen as the what-if scenario clouding Bella's choice, Victoria represents equally disturbing possibilities for Edward if anything were to happen to Bella. "Vampires view their situation as a blessing or a curse, and we see both sides of it," says Bryce.

And playing opposite Robert Pattinson, ultimately? "Rob just does not take himself seriously," says Bryce. "He's just a total sweetheart goof, very humble, and adorable in that way." ■

VICTORIA JUMPS ONTO THE BOAT!

> 66 Bryce was amazing: extremely professional, down-to-earth, very funny, and probably the hardest-working person I've ever met in my life. 99
> —XAVIER SAMUEL (RILEY)

ON RILEY AND VICTORIA - in an embrace, a dark, discomfiting mirror image of the previous scene. It's sexy, intimate.

RILEY
You're not coming with us?

VICTORIA
It will be a last-minute decision. I told you how it works.

RILEY
(grins)
Right. The Cullens have "powers."

Victoria pulls away, ever-so-slightly irritated by his tone.

VICTORIA
Don't underestimate them, Riley. You'll have the numbers, but they'll be able to anticipate your every move.

RILEY
According to your friend.

She looks at him, not sure where he's going with this. She circles him --

VICTORIA
Yes, my *dead* friend. Laurent found out about the things they could do and they killed him. But not before he told me.

RILEY
(carefully)
Maybe he was wrong.
(off her look)
I mean, this is supposed to be Cullen territory. But we've been tearing it up and I've never even seen them here --

Fury flashes in Victoria's eyes. She's suddenly standing several feet away from him.

VICTORIA
You don't trust me.

RILEY
With my life. I'm just saying that --

VICTORIA
(emotional)
I'm doing this for *us*. So we can feed without their retaliation. I can't live in fear anymore, waiting for them to attack --

89

Kristen and Taylor getting ready to shoot a scene for ECLIPSE

MEET THE QUILEUTES

One of the biggest contributions the *Twilight* films have made to the cultural dialogue lies in their portrayal of contemporary Native Americans. In the world of *Twilight*, they may sometimes be wary antagonists of the vampires in their midst, but at heart they are people with a distinguished history, who have vibrant, integrated lives in today's world. For Chaske Spencer, who lived on reservations in Montana and Idaho growing up and is of the Lakota Sioux tribe, busting up the Hollywood stereotype of the "savage"—or the "leather and feather" image often seen in period pieces— was one of the best parts of playing Sam Uley. "I'm really proud of the fact that for *Twilight*, we didn't have to do any of that," says Chaske, who credits *New Moon* director Chris Weitz for emphasizing character over type. "He wanted us to just be regular, normal people, to make us human more than anything else."

A casting mantra for Chris Weitz, in fact, was putting Native Americans or Native Canadians in roles wherever possible. "We were able to cast out of the First Nations," he says. "And that was important."

Among the actors playing shape-shifting Quileutes, Kiowa Gordon (Embry Call) is Hualapai, Bronson Pelletier (Jared Cameron) comes from the Plains Cree, Julia Jones (Leah Clearwater) is part Chickasaw and Choctaw, and Alex Meraz (Paul Lahote) hails from the Purepecha tribe.

Canadian-born Cree descendant Tyson Houseman, who plays Quil Ateara, likes that the movies turn the "stoic dude in a headdress" depiction on its ear by presenting a "different take on it, young guys who are cool, active, and funny. A lot of the Native American fan bases, they see us as huge role models, which is really cool."

"When I go on a reservation, it's a pretty big deal for some of these kids to see this," says Chaske. "When I was a kid, it was *Star Wars*. For these kids, it's *Twilight*. It's really made me grateful and given me an understanding of how powerful the medium is."

Comanche actor Gil Birmingham (Billy Black) is impressed with how the *Twilight* films fuse elements of Native American beliefs into the story's fantastical modern-day narrative in ways that enhance the understanding and appreciation of both. "It incorporates the culture in a very positive sense," says Gil, "to the extent that the werewolves, the only reason they transformed was that they were protective of their people, and protecting their land, which really gets to the root of most Native American culture." ➤

Gil Birmingham as
BILLY BLACK

G il Birmingham got his first inkling of what it might mean to be a part of *Twilight* when, after it was announced he would be playing Jacob's father, Billy Black, the actor's website crashed. "My webmaster called and asked what was going on," recalls Gil. "We had eleven thousand hits in two hours!"

When Gil reflects on the days of *Twilight*, shooting in Portland with actors who weren't megastars yet, he can't believe now that times were once that simple. "We didn't have the pressure, just the freedom to be able to hang out and go to dinner every night and just be ourselves," says Gil. "To enjoy each other's company."

In his approach to playing Billy, Gil took some of the natural camaraderie he felt with actors Billy Burke, who played best buddy Charlie Swan, and Taylor Lautner, as Jacob, and imbued his character, who uses a wheelchair, with a fun-loving side. "I think I brought a lot of my own jovial personality to it, which is not exactly the way it was portrayed in the book. It had more to do with how much fun we had with the material. Fake fighting with Billy, the 'keeping it real' line, those quirks. It was all very sweet."

Staying in a wheelchair during all the movies was surprisingly easy, he adds. "It turned out to be a rather comfortable position to be in for the subsequent movies, because we were working twelve- to fourteen-hour days, and I always had a seat!" ∎

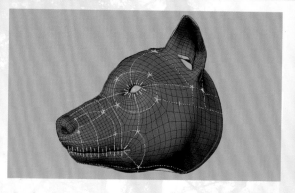

For the gifted animators at Tippett Studio, one challenge with rendering the wolves wasn't merely getting wolf movement right, but scaling the size upward so the wolves were believable as horse-sized canines. "We've done a lot of work with our muscle system to get just the right amount of mass and follow-through," says Tippett art director Nate Fredenburg. "On top of the animation, we've done effects tricks to get the fur to move and have the weight you would want to see in something that large." As for musculature,

the wolves' heavy pelt meant that every layer of under-the-skin muscle didn't have to be rendered. "We've learned to be strategic and to pick and choose key muscle groups or masses within the body that tend to have secondary movement that you would actually see," says Nate. "Think of fur as just a big blur filter. It tends to deaden any of those visual cues. There are a lot of smaller muscles that have an important job, but they don't visually add to the movement."

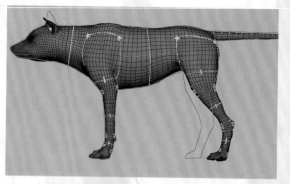

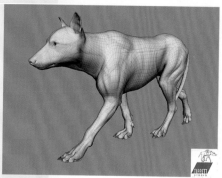

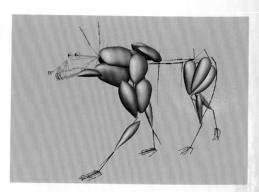

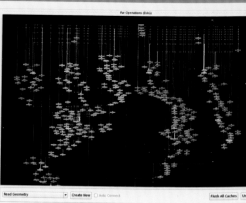

With each successive movie, Tippett Studio had to do more computer-generated shots, from sixty in *New Moon* to the nearly 150 in *Breaking Dawn - Part 1*, and they've gone from creating only six wolves for *New Moon* to sixteen for *Breaking Dawn - Part 2*. And with advancements in Tippett's own fur-generating tool, called Furator (originally called Furrocious), between *New Moon* and *Eclipse* the number of hairs on individual wolves also increased, from three million hairs per animal to around ten million. Computer-processing power has natural constraints on how many hairs can be calculated, but Tippett's new technology could clone their hair clumps. "Wolves have really thick pelts," says Tippett art director Nate Fredenburg. "And though we can't grow enough hairs to replicate how many are on real wolves, our tool allows us to groom and do things that help it feel lusher and thicker than it actually is. It's all about trying to get a better-looking wolf." Adds Phil Tippett, "Hundreds and hundreds of man-hours go into trying to get the right sheen, color, texture, and crinkle. So many moving parts!"

> The effects people also had to accommodate directors who wanted to put their stamp on how the wolves came off overall. Chris, for example, sought an anthropomorphized creature whose human majesty was identifiable. *Breaking Dawn* director Bill Condon, however, asked for a rangier, more "lived-in" wolf, says Phil. "It's been a great opportunity to have this franchise," says Phil. "Just to be able to refine our techniques and processes on the technical side. Usually, by the time you get to the end of the movie, and it's finished, you've finally figured out how to do it. So just having another movie so you can take it to the next level—like how the fur looks—is great."

What's been important to remember, says *Breaking Dawn - Part 2* visual effects supervisor Terry Windell, is that the audience for the *Twilight* movies is different from that for the average effects movie. "Nowadays most effects films have to do with the volume of the spectacle they're trying to create," says Terry. "What's unique about the *Twilight* films is there's much more consideration to the design and elegance of the shot, and that most of the effects should be transparent. Effects are there to support the story and the characters. And I think this audience appreciates a much more elegant process." ■

Mackenzie Foy on a mechanical Jacob-wolf that will be
digitally rendered later, for BREAKING DAWN - PART 2

incredible at what he does."

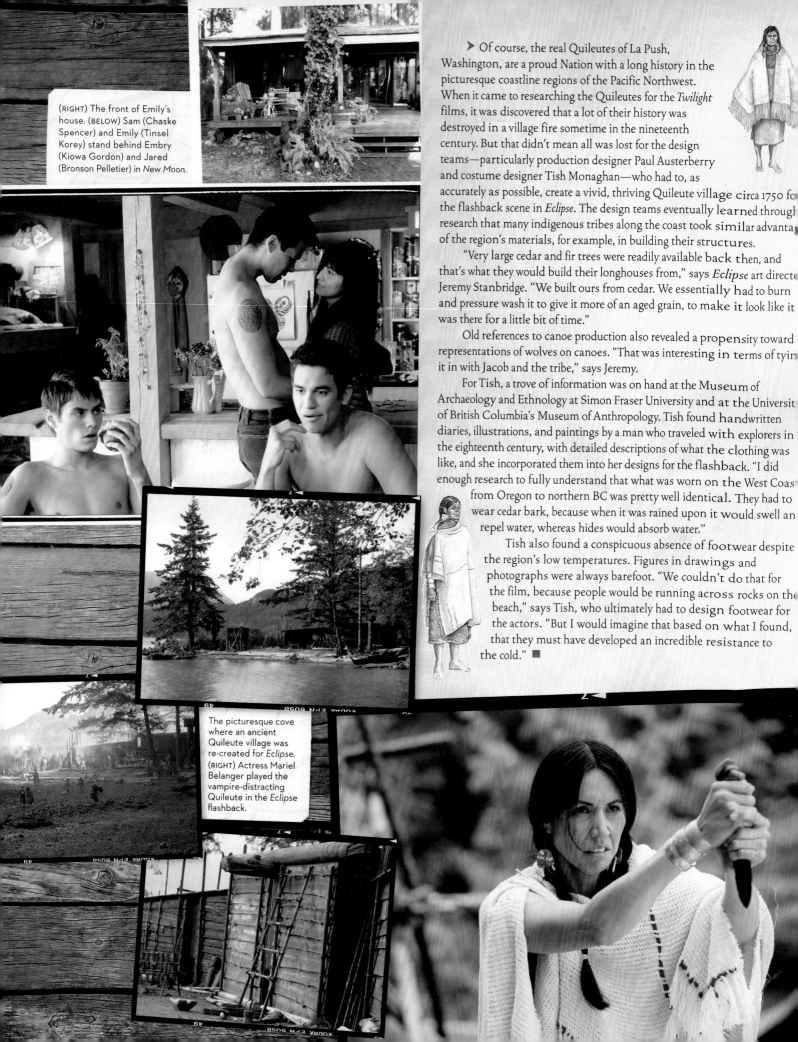

(RIGHT) The front of Emily's house. (BELOW) Sam (Chaske Spencer) and Emily (Tinsel Korey) stand behind Embry (Kiowa Gordon) and Jared (Bronson Pelletier) in *New Moon*.

The picturesque cove where an ancient Quileute village was re-created for *Eclipse*. (RIGHT) Actress Mariel Belanger played the vampire-distracting Quileute in the *Eclipse* flashback.

➤ Of course, the real Quileutes of La Push, Washington, are a proud Nation with a long history in the picturesque coastline regions of the Pacific Northwest. When it came to researching the Quileutes for the *Twilight* films, it was discovered that a lot of their history was destroyed in a village fire sometime in the nineteenth century. But that didn't mean all was lost for the design teams—particularly production designer Paul Austerberry and costume designer Tish Monaghan—who had to, as accurately as possible, create a vivid, thriving Quileute village circa 1750 for the flashback scene in *Eclipse*. The design teams eventually learned through research that many indigenous tribes along the coast took similar advantage of the region's materials, for example, in building their structures.

"Very large cedar and fir trees were readily available back then, and that's what they would build their longhouses from," says *Eclipse* art director Jeremy Stanbridge. "We built ours from cedar. We essentially had to burn and pressure wash it to give it more of an aged grain, to make it look like it was there for a little bit of time."

Old references to canoe production also revealed a propensity toward representations of wolves on canoes. "That was interesting in terms of tying it in with Jacob and the tribe," says Jeremy.

For Tish, a trove of information was on hand at the Museum of Archaeology and Ethnology at Simon Fraser University and at the University of British Columbia's Museum of Anthropology. Tish found handwritten diaries, illustrations, and paintings by a man who traveled with explorers in the eighteenth century, with detailed descriptions of what the clothing was like, and she incorporated them into her designs for the flashback. "I did enough research to fully understand that what was worn on the West Coast from Oregon to northern BC was pretty well identical. They had to wear cedar bark, because when it was rained upon it would swell and repel water, whereas hides would absorb water."

Tish also found a conspicuous absence of footwear despite the region's low temperatures. Figures in drawings and photographs were always barefoot. "We couldn't do that for the film, because people would be running across rocks on the beach," says Tish, who ultimately had to design footwear for the actors. "But I would imagine that based on what I found, that they must have developed an incredible resistance to the cold." ■

(ABOVE) Billy Burke, Alex Rice, Gil Birmingham, and Taylor Lautner in *Breaking Dawn - Part 1.* (BELOW) Gil, Taylor, and Kristen Stewart on the set of *Breaking Dawn - Part 2.*

Bill Condon (left) directs the shot.

JULIA JONES LOOKS BACK

As fans of the *Twilight* movies know, the wolf-pack members have a special tattoo on their right arms, a circular design with intricate artwork depicting two wolves seemingly baying at each other. Julia Jones, who got to sport one as lone female member Leah Clearwater, recalls one aspect about filming with the tattoo that today makes her cringe a little.

"On the very last day of filming *Breaking Dawn*, I said, 'Does anybody have any idea how I can get this off my arm? It's, like, weird.' Well, Taylor Lautner looked at me like, 'Are you crazy? Are you kidding me? They take it off after every day with alcohol!' I never realized that. I was just letting it fall off after three or four days at a time, which had been a real pain. So yeah, that made me feel pretty stupid."

STUNTS

What would a *Twilight* movie be without memorable stuntwork? From the pulleys and winches that allowed Robert Pattinson's and Kristen Stewart's stunt doubles to look like they were climbing sky-jabbing trees in the first movie, to the extensively choreographed Volturi-Cullens melee that reaches an action crescendo in *The Twilight Saga: Breaking Dawn - Part 2*, physical prowess on the part of vampires or shape-shifters has been a hallmark of the series.

When your actors are itching to do as many of their own stunts as possible, it can get worrisome for producers. Taylor Lautner and Kellan Lutz are perhaps *Twilight*'s two biggest daredevils, but it was Kristen who broke her thumb while shooting second-unit fight shots for *Part 2*. "She had to wear a splint for most of the rest of the [shoot]," says producer Wyck Godfrey. "She's got a splint on in the wedding." Thankfully, it could be removed digitally in postproduction, but it's a lesson in mitigating actor eagerness, he notes. "Kristen loves shooting action, but I think she goes into it with such excitement that sometimes she gets hurt doing it."

For the grueling fight between Volturi guard member Felix (Daniel Cudmore) and Edward in *New Moon*, Daniel said he and Rob had fun mapping out the logistics with stunt coordinator J. J. Makaro, but when filming time came, it was sometimes a different ball game. "The thing that worked perfectly when you had a T-shirt on suddenly is not working that well in beautifully tailor-made jacket and pants," says Daniel, laughing. "So you've really got to step it up. I think I split three pairs of pants."

Before *Breaking Dawn*, *Eclipse* featured the most action, since it also climaxed in a battle, between the allied Cullens and werewolves against the newborns. Nikki Reed, who cops to a love for stunt training, recalls how fortuitous it was that she quit smoking right before stunt training for *Eclipse*. "None of us had any idea that we were going to be in a six-week boot camp," she recalls. "The last three years of my life, doing these movies, have been awesome now that I don't smoke, because I've been very involved physically."

One of the series' most-used stunt rigs has been the "magic carpet," which helps simulate vampires' sleek, elegant, and rapid foot speed. Before it changed to a conveyor belt hauled by a truck, actors were pulled on a sheet of Plexiglas covered by leaves, a setup that Cam Gigandet—who took the carpet ride as James in *Twilight* alongside costars Edi Gathegi and Rachelle Lefevre—likens to "speed walking on the flat escalator at the airport." Learning to do it wasn't easy, he says. "We were practicing for hours, trying to look cool, like we knew what we were doing. But that thing was going twenty miles an hour. It was a comedy of errors. But hey, I feel totally at ease at the airport now!"

Judi Shekoni, who plays Amazonian vampire Zafrina in *Breaking Dawn - Part 2*, describes her own stunt follies trying to nail down her grand entrance with Tracey Heggins, who plays coven pal Senna. "They put us about forty feet up in the air, and then they would drop us, the idea being that we would land in this real animalistic, vampire way," says Judi. "But the problem was, every time they dropped us, I went, 'Aaaaaah!' I mean, everybody's looking concerned, and it took me a good five times of screaming and throwing my arms before I realized I had to try to be in character. So I just kept thinking, 'I'm Zafrina! I'm Zafrina!' Then I could do it. But until then, I was acting like I was on a roller coaster at Six Flags." ■

The splint that had to be digitally removed

(ABOVE) Wire and harness protect Jackson Rathbone's stunt double in *Eclipse*.

➤ Emmett's the guy who really digs being a vampire, says Kellan, who took that approach to his moments on film. "He doesn't think it's a bad thing. He was dying, and Rosalie saved his life, and he thinks it's cool.... Now he has superpowers and can hunt anything."

Over the course of five movies, the brawniest of the Cullen actors says his favorite part was the stuntwork, although making the other actors laugh was a close second. "I loved his one-liners," he says. "In *Twilight*, when I'm raising that knife and I say, 'Well, her name is Bella,' having Nikki Reed turn and just crack up like she couldn't contain herself—that was the most fun."

Mostly, Kellan feels fortunate to have been a part of such a popular, beloved franchise, from the moviemaking itself to the fans he treasures. "It's really something special that I'll be able to share for the rest of my life with my kids and grandkids. I wouldn't trade it for the world." ■

> ❝ Kellan's super silly all the time. Either he's being silly, or he's doing so many push-ups that we're all laughing and he doesn't know he's being silly. There's always something. ❞ —NIKKI REED (ROSALIE)

Jackson Rathbone as
JASPER HALE

Yes, indeed, Jessica: When we first glimpse Jasper traversing the high school cafeteria, he looks like he is in pain. And Jackson Rathbone thinks that's what adheres Twilight fans to the moodiest of Cullen vampires. "They're into the fact that Jasper has a dark backstory," says Jackson. "And that's the thing that really popped him off the page to me."

Knowing that Anna Kendrick's Jessica was going to have that "pain" description hovering over Jasper's first appearance, Jackson had to figure out how to play that. "Then it hit me," he says, recalling what he felt when he got the role and discovered a Cullen wasn't a typical dead man vamping. "It was the idea of, 'I'm playing a vampire but I don't have teeth and I don't get to kill people?'" So Jackson transferred that measured disappointment to Jasper: "I decided to play him as, 'I could rip through this entire lunchroom and have a feast and love it, but I can't for moralistic and love-invoked reasons.'"

That was just for the first movie, however. After Jasper's attack on Bella at the beginning of *New Moon*—the filming of which Jackson loved ("Vampires are bloodthirsty, so it's fun to get a little of that action in there")—Jackson approached him as "remorseful, almost beaten down, and that carried through to *Eclipse* until Jasper had to step up and teach the family something he loved, which was battle. He missed that aspect of war. Suddenly he's doing it for justified reasons again, and that brought him closer to Bella, which is why at the wedding in *Breaking Dawn - Part 1*, it's the first time we ever get to see Jasper smile."

Needless to say, Jackson loved shooting Jasper's vampire origins in *Eclipse*, since it was that passage in the third book that initially helped Jackson play Jasper for *Twilight*. But also, he notes, "I grew up riding as a kid, so I got to ride a horse down into this canyon and meet these three beautiful vampires who seduce and then turn Jasper," he says. "Then I got to be the ravenous vampire monster I'd always wanted to play!" ∎

(ABOVE AND RIGHT) Filming the birthday scene in *New Moon* when Jasper attacks Bella

EXT. DESERT OUTSIDE HOUSTON, TEXAS - NIGHT (1863)

MATCH CUT - JASPER'S HUMAN FACE, tan and flushed with the
exertion of riding his horse full throttle down the dirt
road. He looks dashing in his Confederate uniform.

                    JASPER (V.O.)
    I was riding back to Galveston after evacuating a column of
           women and children... when I saw them...

He slows when he sees THREE WOMEN in frayed dresses and
bare feet. Their beauty overwhelms him. MARIA, Mexican,
black-haired, porcelain-skinned, is flanked by two blondes,
LUCY and NETTIE. He dismounts, politely bows. Maria
scrutinizes him.

                    JASPER (V.O.)
    Southern gentleman that I was, I immediately offered her
                         aid.

                    LUCY
               (inhaling his scent)
           Mmm. Lovely. And an officer.

                    NETTIE
           You'd better do it, Maria. I can
           never stop once I've started.

Jasper is confused but mesmerized as Maria moves closer.

                    MARIA
           What's your name, soldier?

                    JASPER
           Major Jasper Whitlock, ma'am.

                    MARIA
    I hope you survive. You may be of great use to me.

FAN BITES:
CAST MEMBERS' FAVORITE MEMORIES OF FAN INTERACTIONS

" I'm telling you, the fan base for Twilight, they're so loving. That's the biggest thing. I went to a fan convention in England, and there is zero pretension with Twilight. No one's saying, 'Well, the Klingon word for that is actually . . .' or whatever. This fan base, the foundation is love and raw emotion. It's the human condition, and celebrating that. So when people meet you, they're so joyful. I wasn't sure how I would be received at this convention, because there's no footage of me yet, and I'm minimally listed in the book. But when they said, 'Presenting Mary . . . Toni Trucks!' people were ripping out their hair, screaming, throwing things. I just was unprepared for the amount of love that I would get just because I was in proximity to characters and actors that they loved and had known. " —TONI TRUCKS (MARY)

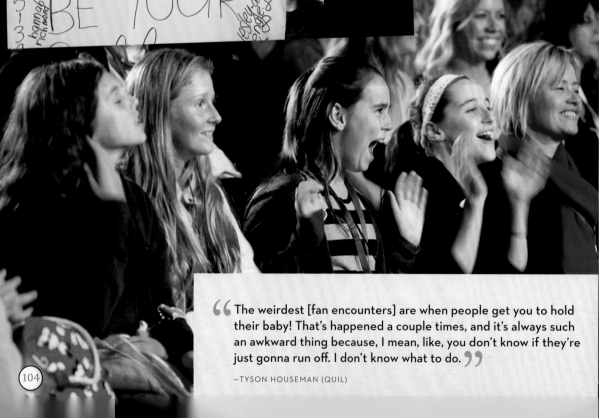

" The weirdest [fan encounters] are when people get you to hold their baby! That's happened a couple times, and it's always such an awkward thing because, I mean, like, you don't know if they're just gonna run off. I don't know what to do. "
—TYSON HOUSEMAN (QUIL)

" Because I knew I was going to be going back and forth over the border to Canada so many times, I went to get something called a Nexus pass, where you register with customs, go through all this screening, so you can go through customs faster later. But they really grill you at customs, because they don't want to make it easy, obviously. And they shouldn't make it easy—they need to really vet you and make sure that nothing fishy is going on, since you won't be talking to a customs officer every time. Well, I went into the customs office, and the woman interviewing me . . . was super intimidating, questioning my paperwork, and I was so nervous I started to stumble, which was freaking me out. Then she looked at my name, looked up at me, and her entire countenance shifted. She said, 'Victoria!' I was like, 'What is happening?' And she just completely changed. This grown woman became a little girl. She told me she'd read the entire TWILIGHT series, again and again and again, started buying all this Twilight paraphernalia and had been putting it up around her house. She said her husband staged an intervention and was like, 'You need to go to therapy. You're a normal woman with children, and what are you doing?' And she was like, 'I can't stop. I'm obsessed. I have dreams about Edward. I don't know what to do. I'm going through a midlife crisis, but I'm really happy about it!' I said, 'Listen, I get it.' Here was this normal woman, a professional who obviously did her job, and the way she completely shifted was so interesting to me. It's like your hormones come alive again. "

—BRYCE DALLAS HOWARD (VICTORIA)

" This girl had designed a Team Peter T-shirt, and it says underneath, 'Because any friend of Jasper is a friend of mine.' She'd put it up on the Internet and she sent me a message saying she'd sold fifty T-shirts, and then at the premiere for *Breaking Dawn - Part 1* I saw a girl, completely unrelated, wearing the T-shirt. I get a kick out of it. You rarely see people get so passionate about anything the way these fans are about this, and it's a nice contrast to the cynicism a lot of other people have. "

—ERIK ODOM (PETER)

Transformation

Breaking Dawn director Bill Condon directing Kristen Stewart and Rob Pattinson in the honeymoon sequence and in the nightmare wedding scene

DIRECTOR'S JOURNAL

BILL CONDON AND
BREAKING DAWN -
PART 1 AND PART 2

Up until the end of ECLIPSE, the TWILIGHT series had thrown more than a handful of obstacles in the path of Bella and Edward. With Stephenie Meyer's final novel BREAKING DAWN giving readers the long-awaited consummation of their love, it seemed the movie version—to be broken into two parts— needed a director who could rally the troops for not just an emotional finish, but one that acknowledged how much its characters had been through.

Enter Oscar-winning filmmaker Bill Condon, who, on his first day with Kristen Stewart and Robert Pattinson, asked them what you'd have if you took the vampires and werewolves out of the script. As Bill recalls, "I said, 'What would it be about?' Well, it's about how *Twilight* grows up. It's all been about fantasy up until now, and now it's the reality of the first year of a marriage, where you've gotten what you wanted, you're now living with him or her, and this is what they really are. This is what their value system is."

With *The Twilight Saga: Breaking Dawn - Part 1* kicking off with the happy day but ultimately centered on Bella's pregnancy and the rift she and Edward have over its effect on her health, Bill sought a dramatic thrust to the narrative that was determined by his two leads, not outside forces. "I just kept trying to keep in front of that with adult concerns, and I think Kristen and Rob were into that. But I think that's who they are, too. They've grown up fast." ➤

Bill Condon directing Taylor Lautner

Kristen recognized in Bill a fellow fan. "It was like, 'Oh, you love it like I love it!'" she recalls telling him. "That's what we needed. Generally, he put the story back into Bella's head. We'd started slipping away from that, but he found the heart in it again. It got hot again, and it had started to feel cold to me. So it was really like, 'Thank God!'"

Bill even knew about the mysterious dog painting that had been a prop staple of Bella's bedroom since *Twilight*. "Bill loves that thing," says Kristen. "He said, 'Yeah, I saw them carting it out, and I told them to put it right back.' And I was like, 'See, that is why you belong here. That is the coolest thing that you know that.'"

Bill Condon, Rami Malek (Benjamin), and Angela Sarafyan (Tia)

Bill's reputation with actors is famously strong, having directed Ian McKellen, Laura Linney, and Eddie Murphy to Oscar nominations, and guided Jennifer Hudson to her Oscar win for *Dreamgirls*. Praise for him from the *Twilight* cast has been across-the-board laudatory. "It must always be difficult for someone coming onto a film who hasn't been a part of it from the beginning," says Michael Sheen. "But Bill is so friendly and a warm presence on set. He was thoroughly enjoyable to work for. The franchise has been very lucky." ➤

Bill directing Taylor and Kristen in PART 2

⚬ PRODUCER'S DIARY ⚬

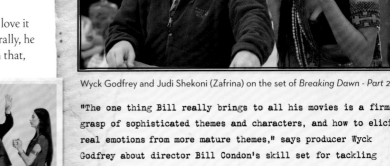

Wyck Godfrey and Judi Shekoni (Zafrina) on the set of *Breaking Dawn - Part 2*

"The one thing Bill really brings to all his movies is a firm grasp of sophisticated themes and characters, and how to elicit real emotions from more mature themes," says producer Wyck Godfrey about director Bill Condon's skill set for tackling *The Twilight Saga: Breaking Dawn - Part 1* and *Part 2*. "He is a storyteller first and foremost, he's a writer, he believes strongly in the dramatization of human character through action, and so he really focused hard on the scripts to make sure Melissa Rosenberg told a story of how once you get married, things aren't over. Relationships become complicated."

BREAKING DAWN was an uncomfortable novel for a lot of the series' younger fans, says Wyck. "For a lot of readers, they hadn't gone through those things: married at eighteen, immediately pregnant, having a baby, and then marital strife. For our actors, too, they were having to play characters going through life events they hadn't gone through, either."

Wyck praises Bill's ability to connect with actors in a way that zeroes in on the emotional heart of a scene. "With the least amount of external action and the most internal and relationship conflict of any of the movies, we needed a director like Bill for *Part 1*." Robert Pattinson, in particular, relished the chance to show the anguish of disagreeing with Bella's decision to go through a potentially life-threatening birth. "You really got to see his frustration that she made a decision without him, and Bill did a great job of pulling that out."

> The combined one-hundred-day shoot for *The Twilight Saga: Breaking Dawn - Part 1* and *Part 2* meant that Bill often had to mentally juggle between scenes for different films. Shooting the final half-hour-long showdown between the Cullens and the Volturi for *Part 2*, however, was epically all-inclusive: nearly his entire cast—dozens of vampires—on a makeshift field of fake snow and greenscreen walls for over a month, either talking, standing around, or fighting.

"It was this incredible puzzle," says Bill, who instead of trying to figure out all the steps, moves, and camera shots in front of waiting actors, took a day off from filming so he and the crew could walk through the sequence—the dialogue, the reaction shots, and the action—like a play rehearsal. "Beat by beat, that's what we did, and it was fascinating. And out of that came a lot of lovely compositions and moments."

Before all that, however, Bill's experience as a screenwriter—his Oscar came for the 1998 film *Gods and Monsters*—came in handy as well. Melissa Rosenberg, who worked closely with Bill in getting the *Breaking Dawn* scripts into shape, applauds his storytelling gifts and emphasis on character. Says Melissa, "He made me a better writer. And after a twenty-year career, that's saying a lot!"

As immersed as Bill became in the *Twilight* world, it was going to the premiere of *Part 1* and watching it with a crowd full of fans that both reminded him of how big the phenomenon was—"like a Beatles concert," he says—and clued him in to how accepted he was as a conduit for Stephenie's story. Anticipation of the reaction to Jacob's imprinting alone—a controversial enough idea already in the fan world—had been enough to worry him. Until the scene came, and Bill's idea to have Taylor Lautner fall to his knees as he approaches the baby Renesmee drew a round of applause.

"I have to say," he adds, "that was one of the most pleasurable moments I've had watching a movie." ■

(ABOVE AND RIGHT) Scenes from *Breaking Dawn - Part 2.* (BELOW) Wyck Godfrey and Bill Condon.

"Anything with Edward Cullen. Anything where they're making out and then he needs to abstain from either killing her or consuming her. I remember when I saw *Breaking Dawn - Part 1*, and he broke the bed, I was just dying. Dying! My husband was like, 'What are you, fourteen?' (Laughs) I said, 'No, I'm a hormonal pregnant thirty-year-old woman, okay? Just give this to me, let me have this!'" —Bryce Dallas Howard (Victoria)

"One scene sticks out in my head, and it broke my heart. When Bella died in *Breaking Dawn - Part 1*, and Edward was trying to revive her and bite her back to life, it was sick but sweet all at the same time. His desperation and his heart, he didn't want to believe it. If my loved one was dying, I wouldn't want to believe it, either. He was like, 'No, she's not dead.' And it took a while. I think there was thirty seconds of that, and I thought, *Wow.* It touched my heart." —Tracey Heggins (Senna)

(LEFT) Artist's rendering of what the broken honeymoon bed should look like. (ABOVE) The actual "destroyed" bed on set.

"My favorite scene is that birth scene. I thought it was awesome! I felt like they really kept it in the tone of the films that have come before, but they also managed to go there, where the book goes, and they didn't trivialize it. It's awesome and gory and surprising and disconcerting and kind of epic. And I think that's what the books are about in a way. It's about these things that are bigger than life, and it's hard to put it on-screen, but I think they did it." —Marlane Barnes (Maggie)

FROM PAGE TO SCREEN
ADAPTING BREAKING DAWN

T he TWILIGHT novels aren't exactly slim volumes, so when it came to turning the fourth book into a film, the subject of whether it should be one or two movies was broached. At first, Melissa Rosenberg and Stephenie Meyer thought it was a single, very packed movie. "But I said I'd go and break it down and see if there's two," says Melissa. "And it became clear very quickly it was two. There's just way too much information, too much story for one movie."

For *The Twilight Saga: Breaking Dawn - Part 1*, a wedding, a honeymoon, and a birth all contribute to a greater sense of intimacy than in any of the films prior. Yet apart from the terror surrounding Bella's pregnancy, to Melissa, there lacked an exterior threat. She considered bringing in the Volturi but, realizing they were needed for *The Twilight Saga: Breaking Dawn - Part 2*, discarded that idea after a few drafts. That's when, in consultation with director Bill Condon, she turned to the section written from Jacob's point of view, and the two saw a way to extrapolate the tension. "In the book, there's all this stuff going on with Jacob and his pack, and the threat of the pack wanting to kill the baby," says Melissa. "So it was really about pulling that forward. And Jacob's story, about breaking off and forming his own pack, becoming his own man, is in line with Bella becoming her own woman." ➤

(ABOVE) Tyson Houseman, Kiowa Gordon, Bronson Pelletier, and Alex Meraz. (RIGHT) Booboo Stewart, Julia Jones, and Taylor Lautner. (BELOW) Julia and Taylor in *Breaking Dawn - Part 1*.

(TOP TO BOTTOM) Charlie Swan (Billy Burke) walking his daughter down the aisle; lighting the wedding in the woods of Squamish, British Columbia; Bella's bouquet, made of hyacinth, freesia, larkspur, and ranunculus.

THE WEDDING:
A CEREMONY THEY'LL NEVER FORGET

If there's one thing that the actors who participated in the filming of Bella and Edward's wedding can agree on, it's that the vibe was that of a real nuptial, especially in the emotions it brought forth.

"That was very surreal, actually," recalls Christian Camargo, who plays Denali coven member Eleazar. "You know it's a production, but you can't help but get swept up in the fantasy of it. And when the cameras started rolling, I didn't realize she was walking down the aisle. I thought that would be a different setup. So we just turned, and all of a sudden Kristen's in her wedding dress walking down the aisle in the most incredible setting. I've never experienced that on a movie before, where reality and fantasy blurred."

Elizabeth Reaser remembers being with Kristen before the scene was filmed and sensing a real bride's big-day jitters. "She was actually nervous, which was really sweet and cute," says Elizabeth. "That was moving to me because you don't often see that."

Production designer Richard Sherman's set evoked a ceremony seemingly born of the forest where it took place, à la *A Midsummer Night's Dream*, with everything draped in moss and flora and an aisle carpeted in tiny blue-and-white flowers. "It turned out very well," says Richard. "That was fun to do." ➤

Bella and her parents pre-wedding in PART 1

THE NIGHTMARE DRESS

For Bella's nightmare nuptials, in which her moment at the altar turns into a bloody vision of carnage, the dress also had to reflect the kind of experience our heroine wouldn't want.

"We wanted a dress that didn't match her personality," says *Breaking Dawn* costume designer Michael Wilkinson. "So it had the bare shoulders, all that bare skin, the tight bodice, the big poofy ball-gown skirt, very antithetical to her jeans-and-T-shirt style of dressing."

Michael remembers Kristen Stewart openly complaining about the veil that was part of the dress, too. "She was so thrown by the veil, saying, 'I don't get veils. Why do brides have to wear veils? It's so weird!' So I think we succeeded in making her feel kind of nightmarish and uncomfortable!"

> Of course, filming in British Columbia—woodsy Squamish, specifically—rain was a concern. "We were worried, how are they going to make this epic wedding seem 'epic' in the rain?" recalls Sarah Clarke, who plays Bella's mom, Renée. "But then the clouds broke open and the sun came out for that day. It was freezing, but everything glistened and sort of sparkled, and even though you were cold, you just had to take in the magnificence of it."

For Christian Serratos, who plays Angela, the fan in her looked around that day and knew audiences would be happy with the long-awaited moment. "I read all the books, so when I saw the wedding, I was so thrilled and knew every other fan would be. I remember all the girls were talking about how when our wedding day comes, how it'd be a better move to get set decorators than actual wedding planners!"

Security may have been particularly intense for the filming of the scene, between the umbrellas shielding the Carolina Herrera wedding dress and the no-cell-phone rule, and the routine interruptions of choppers overhead trying to get pictures, but it also added to the sense that something special was happening. "It will never be repeated, and that's exactly the way it should be," adds Christian Camargo.

Billy Burke, whose Charlie Swan memorably beamed with a sense of understated pride, sums up the shooting experience this way: "Something was happening that day. I can't really explain it, but it kind of came over me, and I think it came over quite a few of the actors. But it was the culmination of everything, and it was kind of magical. For all the pomp and circumstance, it felt like we were doing something that was part of Hollywood history. I'll remember that for a while." ∎

THE WEDDING DRESS

Bella and Edward's wedding would become one of the most anticipated events in the franchise. Creating the perfect wedding dress was crucial, and the question was how to make it elegant, young, vintage, and sexy all at the same time. Designer Carolina Herrera had the answer: long sleeves combined with a sheer Chantilly lace back, clean lines augmented by a dazzling row of buttons down the spine, crepe satin with a silk-thread topstitch.

Known for the femininity and timeless quality of her creations, Carolina Herrera was the ideal designer for the job. "What I have been doing all these years is trying to make women feel more beautiful," she says. Born in Caracas, Venezuela, she began designing clothes in 1980 with the encouragement of legendary *Vogue* editor Diana Vreeland. Carolina founded her label in New York in 1981, and today she is internationally renowned for her fashions and fragrances—top celebrities such as Renée Zellweger, Emily Blunt, and Jessica Alba often walk the red carpet in her gowns.

Summit executive Gillian Bohrer recalls the first time Kristen Stewart tried on the wedding dress: "It was stunning. It fit her like a glove. I love that dress. It manages to be daring and slightly risqué in a way that's completely tasteful and elegant."

In the novel BREAKING DAWN, Bella doesn't see herself in the dress until Edward points out her reflection in a window after they exchange vows. That wasn't going to work as a point-of-view technique on film—a wedding scene where the audience can't see the dress?! So the filmmakers paid tribute in their own way. As Bella walks down the aisle, we get tantalizing details—the shoes, some of the lace-and-button detail on the back—and then she stops to see Edward on the altar smiling back at her. "When we cut to Edward's point of view, that's the first time you see Kristen fully revealed in this amazing dress," notes Gillian. "And that moment got gasps, which was nice." ■

Wedding dress designer Carolina Herrera

" There were three fittings with Kristen, and when she initially put on the dress and looked over her shoulder into the mirror, she was very moved. In that moment, she was not an actress or a character in a film; she was a bride, and a happy one at that. It is always very important to make the bride happy, of course, and in this case I was delighted to do so. It was a very special moment for both Kristen and the character of Bella to share. " —CAROLINA HERRERA

BELLA
BREAKING DAWN
twilight saga
costume design: michael wilkinson
illustration: phil boutte and mw

BELLA
BREAKING DAWN
twilight saga
costume design: michael wilkinson
illustration: phil boutte and mw

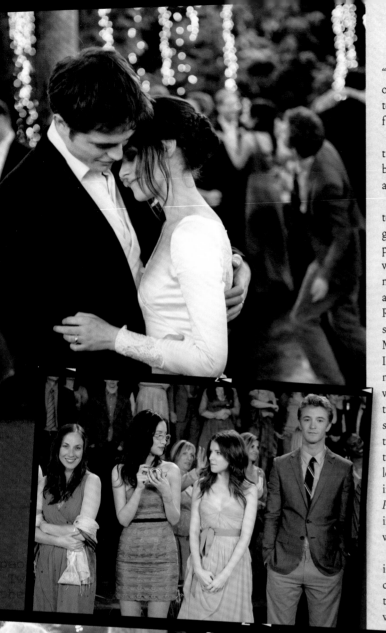

▶ The wedding, meanwhile, provided room for a screenwriter's touch. "In the book, it's very much from Bella's point of view, and it kind of glosses over in a dream. But we want to see the specifics of the wedding. We want to see the toasts, people dancing, Mike getting wild out there on the dance floor, which is actually in the script."

Melissa relished the chance to get in some humor, too, from writing the toasts to Jessica's gossipy speculation that Bella is getting married because she's expecting. "One of my favorite lines is 'Who else gets married at eighteen?' That stuff is fun because that's what we're thinking!"

A guest was added, too, to help lay the groundwork for the key plot point of *Part 2*, when Denali coven member Irina sees Bella and Edward's daughter, Renesmee, and assumes she's an immortal child. Melissa felt that given Irina's history in the mythology (her boyfriend was Laurent, killed by the wolves in *New Moon*), seeing her for the first time in *Part 2* would feel too sudden. "I thought, let's introduce her, and introduce her conflict, in *Part 1*. In the book, Irina is not at the wedding, so I put her there. I felt it was important [as] a setup for the second movie. It also led to another line I like, when Edward says, 'What's a wedding without a little family drama?'"

Stephenie Meyer and Wyck Godfrey, who have cameos in the wedding scene

Though BREAKING DAWN had, of course, been published, it wasn't initially certain that Stephenie would sell the film rights to it if the story's conclusion—a tense showdown between the Volturi and the Cullens with their friends—wasn't kept the way it goes down in the book. "She didn't want it to be what it's not," says Melissa empathetically. "She didn't want anyone killed who does not get killed."

But in talking through the possibilities, it was the strength of Stephenie's characters that ultimately spelled out a solution—one that allowed for *Breaking Dawn* to build to its justifiably tense, visceral, and cathartic end. ■

(ABOVE LEFT) The newlyweds.
(MIDDLE) Bella's human guests.
(BOTTOM) Bella and Edward flanked by members of the Denali coven.

ISABELLA MARIE SWAN

AND

EDWARD ANTHONY MASEN CULLEN

TOGETHER WITH THEIR FAMILIES
REQUEST THE HONOR OF YOUR PRESENCE
AT THE CELEBRATION OF THEIR MARRIAGE

SATURDAY, THE THIRTEENTH OF AUGUST
TWO THOUSAND AND ELEVEN
FIVE O'CLOCK IN THE EVENING

420 WOODCROFT AVE
FORKS, WA

ROB AND KRISTEN'S
CHEMISTRY

What was quickly apparent when Robert Pattinson and Kristen Stewart play-acted scenes for the *Twilight* video camera over a day and a half at Catherine Hardwicke's Venice Beach house—in every room, outside and inside, even on her bed—was that *Twilight* finally had its species-[...] Catherine afterward that Robert [...] story. "It just felt alive," recalls Erik [...]ment's president of production. "It [...]was chemistry. It was electric. It was [...]real. And it's the kind of thing that you [...]cannot fake. I mean, ultimately, they [...]have become a couple, so I guess they, [...]too, realized they had chemistry. But it [...]was so palpable."

That feeling was reinforced when production on *Twilight* started, and dailies began rolling in. Something about the on-screen space Robert and Kristen shared— the way they stood near each other, talked with each other, made the simplest of gestures—spoke to a magnetic pull. One of the pair might look away during a dialogue scene but still convey where those eyes wished they were directed. [...]t of the lab scene, and I thought, it [...]ll in love," adds Erik. "Even that crazy [...]n you know this is the biggest emotion that has ever existed in the history of mankind." ➤

In speculating on what's behind their chemistry, actress Bryce Dallas Howard, who played Victoria in *The Twilight Saga: Eclipse* and counts herself a dyed-in-the-wool fan of the saga, sees a like-minded pair offscreen and on. "Edward and Bella are people who don't always feel comfortable in their own skin, and have no hubris whatsoever, and [Kristen and Rob] are like that as people themselves," says Bryce. "Those qualities in themselves brought a kind of vulnerability to their characters that translated to the screen. Plus, they both take their work very seriously, so there's going to be really positive results."

It didn't take long for Kristen and Rob to notice that as the movies went along, more and more intimate moments were being written into the scripts. Though the press has had a field day over the years trying to get the pair to acknowledge in public their offscreen romance, there's one way fans of the couple have been able to live vicariously: through their scenes as Bella and Edward. "The funny thing is we're constantly making out in these movies now," says Kristen. "From the third one on, we're constantly kissing! Sometimes it felt a little redundant and weird, especially when every scene is written around the climax of a kiss. It's like 'A-a-a-and . . . here it comes!'"

And why not? Especially if they're the romantic draw of a series of movies based on beloved novels that extol the thrill of eternal love. Simply put, Kristen and Rob sell the idea without coming off like paid showfolk. "The two of them are just so completely natural," says Laura Byrne-Cristiano of the Twilight Lexicon website. "Another set of actors could have sounded really cheesy or might have camped it up. But they just sound unforced. It could be two people you know."

Even more impressive is how the actors helped progress their on-screen relationship, so that by *Breaking Dawn* they'd grown out of the raw emotions of *Twilight* and embodied something richer and deeper: a couple launching themselves into the next phase of their lives. To producer Wyck Godfrey, Kristen and Rob's offscreen chemistry had something to do with that as well.

"Years of having worked together allowed a level of comfort," says Wyck, who witnessed in the pair's final days of shooting—in the Virgin Islands for the ocean lovemaking scene in *The Twilight Saga: Breaking Dawn - Part 1*—an earned maturity. "There was a little bit of I-trust-you, you-trust-me, and it was Edward and Bella at peace with each other. And that's four years of life and experience and working together." ■

The lasting marks of vampire passion . . .

              BELLA
        (putting everything together)
What do you mean, you heard what they were thinking... Are
        you saying you... can read minds?

Edward shrugs. Sheepish.

              BELLA
          (trying to grasp)
Then what am I thinking? Wait -- okay now, go.

              EDWARD
I have no idea. I can read every mind in there, except
yours. (points at other customers) Work, sex, money, sex,
sex, boyfriend -- (points at Bella) Nothing. It's quite
              frustrating.

              BELLA
        Why, what's wrong with me?

              EDWARD
I tell you I read minds and you think there's something
              wrong with you?

He smiles, charmed by her. But his smile fades, that torn
look returns as he watches the waterfall...

              BELLA
            What is it?

              EDWARD
I... don't have the strength to stay away from you anymore.

She's surprised. And *thrilled*.

              BELLA
      Edward, you don't have to.

He's drawn in by her encouraging gaze... but he closes his
eyes a beat, and turns back to the water.

              EDWARD
        (almost to himself)
          This is wrong.

              BELLA
            Edward --

              EDWARD
      You're cold. We should go.

He walks away before she can ask any more questions...

BELLA AND EDWARD'S
COTTAGE

One of the more important sets getting its debut in *The Twilight Saga: Breaking Dawn - Part 2* is the cottage that Alice gives Bella and Edward as a present, a quaint stone hideaway where the vampire couple can live out their love story as a family.

Production designer Richard Sherman's task was twofold: build the thing on a soundstage in Baton Rouge, Louisiana, for the interior scenes; then find a suitably woodsy enclave in the Vancouver, British Columbia, environs for the exterior set. All the while, Richard had to keep in mind the fundamentals as laid out by Stephenie Meyer in the novel, which he interpreted to be "a really cozy, comfortable, womblike place, nestled in the forest with a beautiful garden."

What he came up with was an old-fashioned storybook cottage with a Dutch door, diamond-patterned leaded windows, and a very sloped roofline where the house could "huddle underneath." Finely honed, wide-planked hardwood floors, low-beamed ceilings, and a stone fireplace with stacked wood gave the indoor spaces an intimate feel. Among the many artistic touches, Delft tilework for the fireplace was designed by art director Lorin Flemming. The color scheme included creamy yellows and red, and elsewhere pale gray and powder blue.

A key element for the design team was creating an interior that could be unveiled in a fluid motion by the camera, to approximate someone like Bella going from room to room, looking in wonder at the beauty of new surroundings. "It's like you're coming in the front door, you see the living room and the fire going, and they go straight to Bella's closet that Alice had created for her, then to Renesmee's room, which is every pregnant lady's dream come true, all powder blue and lace and gray, just gorgeous, then into the bedroom. It's very much like in *Part 1*, when she sees the honeymoon house for the first time. It's dictated by the camera, how Bill Condon wanted to reveal the set." ➤

290   CONTINUED: (3)   290

                          ALISTAIR
              We'll see.

Off Bella and Edward sharing an encouraged look...

                          BELLA (V.O.)
              "There is sweet music here..."

291   INT. BELLA & EDWARD'S COTTAGE - NURSERY - NIGHT   291

Bella lies next to Renesmee, (now the size of a 6 yr old)
reading Tennyson to her...

                          BELLA
              ... "That softer falls than petals
              from blown roses on the grass, or
              night dews on still waters..."

She sees Renesmee's eyes shutting.

                          BELLA
              "... Music that brings sweet sleep
              down from the blissful skies...."

Bella closes the book. She reaches for the light when —

                          RENESMEE
              Mom...
                   (off Bella's look)
              Did Aunt Alice and Uncle Jasper run
              away because we're going to die?

Set decorator David Schlesinger sought modern touches when it came to the cottage art.

Becoming
BELLA THE VAMPIRE

One of the final images of *Breaking Dawn - Part 1* was all that moviegoers needed to tantalizingly hint at the supernatural thrills to come in *Part 2*: a newborn Bella opening her eyes to reveal hungrily red orbs. It's an image that meant just as much for Kristen Stewart, because it signified the opportunity for her to play a Bella Swan not simply transformed into a wife and mother, but into a full-on vampire.

"It was amazing," reports Kristen. "I loved it. I'd gotten so stagnant and tight, and I needed to stretch!"

"The expression 'Finally!' is what comes to mind," says MyAnna Buring, whose scenes in *Part 2* as Denali clan member Tanya gave her a firsthand glimpse at Kristen's attitude toward playing a bloodsucking Bella. "She didn't have to hold back, didn't have to be awkward. She could be all cool and move and look incredible. She had a ball."

Producer Wyck Godfrey concurs. "It was fun because she got to play a different character, with a different stature, different control of her voice, and a lot of the nervousness of Bella is replaced with this cool, collected calm of Bella as a vampire. It's no longer her on Edward's back. He's now chasing her, and she's faster."

If there's one thing Kristen had been waiting for, it was to hotfoot it like a vampire through the forest on the special "magic carpet" actors run on while being pulled at forty miles an hour by a truck. "I've watched people do that for years, and I never got a chance to. Actually, it looked terrifying," she recalls. "But I was excited to do it. It definitely feels strange."

For costume designer Michael Wilkinson, *Part 2* is all about Bella's transformation into what her husband has been for a century, and "what sort of physical manifestation it has as far as her choice of clothes, her silhouettes, and the textures and colors she wears."

Since *Part 2* opens with Bella on her first hunt, Michael wanted something "iconic" for her vampiric debut, which also happens to be the outfit the Cullen family has dressed Bella in under the belief that she didn't make it out of the pregnancy alive. "But as she wakes up and becomes a vampire, it's what she races out into the forest in, so it's what we called the hunting dress. It's a tight stretch dress, a striking blue, and it shows off what great shape she's in. It's a color we've never seen her in, so it makes her skin look beautiful. It's a whole fresh feel for vampire Bella." ➤

(TOP TO BOTTOM) A nightstand photo of father and soon-to-be-vampire daughter; Bill Condon directing a scene from *Part 1*; Bella testing her powers with Emmett (Kellan Lutz) in *Part 2*; the vampire couple in *Part 2*.

BELLA
Do you think Jane and Alec have ever had to fight without their
powers?

EDWARD
(looks at her warily)
Probably not... Why?

BELLA
If I'm the only one they can't hurt, I might be able to distract
them --

EDWARD
-- You mean sacrifice yourself.

BELLA
-- I mean fight.

Off Edward dubious, and Bella determined...

EXT. CLEARING BY RIVER - DAY

ON BELLA - an intent expression. Unblinking. Focused. INCLUDE EDWARD
facing her twenty yards across the clearing.

EDWARD
As a newborn, strength is your primary advantage. So strike first
and keep striking.

Bella CHARGES him - all speed and power - lunges for him. He spins,
trips and PINS HER. And is immediately worried --

EDWARD
Are you all right?

BELLA
You can stop asking me that.

She PUSHES him off her, he FLIES back a couple of yards, landing on
his feet. She jumps up, ready for more. WIDEN to reveal Emmett
watching intently . . . Stefan and Vladimir, both amused... Senna

➤ Regarding her m[...]
"The alt-girl tomboy loo[...]
Elizabeth Taylor. Put a lit[...]
and she's a real movie sta[...]

Bella the vampire, i[...]
"since those big, brown [...]
got these spectacular gre[...]
helped transform her face. "It gets her back, in a way, to her natural
beauty," says Condon.

Part 2 also sees Kristen's Bella in more fashionably chic vampire
attire. For her clandestine business meeting in Seattle with J. Jenks,
Michael Wilkinson clad her in "a simple, elegant black dress and a trench
coat," since she's making her only town appearance outside the Cullen
compound. But for the climactic showdown with the Volturi, only a look
of ready-to-fight strength would do. "We had this great leather jacket
made for her, nicely fitted, and it gives her kind of a warrior feel as she
faces the Volturi," says Wilkinson.

In the end, it's only appropriate that the slouchy, lip-biting Bella that
Kristen brought so vividly to the screen in *Twilight* becomes the evolved,
powerful, and family-saving vampire warrior of *Breaking Dawn - Part 2*. It
took a few movies, but the "action geek" in Kristen finally got to do what
she'd seen every other vampire actor do. ▨

Concept art for how
Bella's power manifests
in *Breaking Dawn - Part 2*

FORCES OF NATURE

It's a well-known fact that weather plays an important part in the saga. After all, it's right there on the very first page of the first chapter of the first book: Forks, Washington, where our heroine is headed, is the rainiest place in America, darkened by "gloomy, omnipresent shade."

In reality, the weather made its presence known during every film production. During the forty-two days spent shooting *Twilight* in Portland, Oregon, it often rained, snowed, and even hailed. "It was logistically insane," recalls director Catherine Hardwicke. "There were so many different [weather] scenarios to prepare for."

Things didn't get any easier when production moved to Vancouver for *New Moon* and *Eclipse*. Though the storyline established "a desire to always be in dismal weather," as co-producer Bill Bannerman describes it, this time there was a new group of actors who, whatever the circumstances, needed to look as if they were at a tropical beach resort: the shirtless wolf pack. "It was tough getting through those scenes," admits Chaske Spencer, who plays Sam Uley. "We couldn't show that we were cold. God love the Canadian crews. They would have parkas waiting for us to throw on after each take."

Not that it's necessarily easier for vampire actors to feign indifference to the cold—they're just more likely to be clothed. For a scene at the Denali coven's snow-covered hideaway in *Breaking Dawn - Part 2*, Casey LaBow, who plays Kate, recalls getting approached after a take. "They came up and said, 'Can you not breathe? We can see your breath coming out of your mouth.' That was funny."

The entire *Breaking Dawn* shoot, in fact, was one adaptation to Mother Nature after another. It started in Brazil, where an island residence chosen for its blue skies, green water, and stunning views—all in evidence the first day when the cast and crew showed up, and Kristen and Rob could be found swimming in advance of their honeymoon scenes—became subjected to a cyclone with hundred-mile-an-hour winds and torrential rain by night three.

"It made this incredibly beautiful island look like it was off the coast of Vancouver, as if these poor people brought Forks with them," jokes director Bill Condon, who along with 150-plus people was forced by the Coast Guard to stay at the location house that night, scrounging for food, drink, and a section of floor to sleep on. ➤

Heavy rains turned a beach scene into a mostly van scene in TWILIGHT.

Umbrellas, though sometimes used to shield sets from prying eyes, were often needed because of the weather.

Let it snow, let it snow, let it snow . . . somewhere else!

> Of course, the many months inside soundstages in Baton Rouge, Louisiana, were perfectly controlled, but once filming shifted to Vancouver in February 2011 for the last seven weeks, the production was visited by another meteorological party crasher: snow. The Jacob's-house set, where the first scenes were to be shot, was covered, so the day before filming began, steam crews swooped in and neutralized two-thirds of the offending powder. That stream Jacob jumped over in *New Moon* when he became a wolf? In no time it was overflowing from the melted snow.

The rebuilt Cullen house set up in Squamish had to be tended to next, for fear that branches heavy with snow would crack off and crash through the set. Plus, all the windows meant clearing more than just a small radius. "Acres and acres of forest were steamed," says production designer Richard Sherman. "It was an absolute feat." Bill Bannerman adds, "You know that phrase, 'We moved in when the paint was drying?' Same thing. Everybody walked in going, 'How funny, it didn't snow here!' They had no idea the money we spent."

The wedding scene in *Breaking Dawn*, filmed in April, was subject to a final blast of chilling rain from Vancouver's winter season. Since [these were] supposed to be summertime nuptials, no character—undead or human—could give away the extreme drop in temperature. "It's always cold on a *Twilight* set, but the wedding was something fierce," recalls Christian Serratos, who plays Angela. "We had these insanely cool outfits, but we should have been wearing parkas and earmuffs. Although that wouldn't have looked nearly as pretty."

Christian sums up the costume dilemma of the movies this way: "I remember when we first met with wardrobe on *Twilight*, we were told, 'Look at what's cute, but remember, it's going to be cold out.' I was like, 'Screw that! I'm going to wear what's cute!' We learned our lesson, and by *Breaking Dawn* we all knew: You've got to pick the cutest of the *warmest*." ∎

FAN BITES: MEDIA FRENZY

Nearly every person involved in making the first *Twilight* has their "whoa" moment. For Justin Chon, who plays human classmate Eric, it was walking back to his trailer and being approached by two women beckoning him over. "They said, 'We're part of TwilightMOMS. Here's our card. Call us,'" recalls Justin, laughing. "I had always thought *Twilight* would be a teenage thing, but here were these ladies in their forties. I was like, 'Oh my God, this might be bigger than I think it is, if people are camping out.'"

Websites devoted to Stephenie Meyer's books had been in existence, of course, but interest in the movies expanded the possibilities for media attention, led by enterprising fans armed with all manner of recording devices. (After all, before the mainstream media and the paparazzi went nuts for all things *Twilight*, there were teens with cell phones.) *Twilight* may have been able to shoot in Portland, Oregon, relatively unencumbered by throngs of fans, but as the movies exploded, interest in tracking down filming locations grew.

Line producer Bill Bannerman says the big change was between the Vancouver, British Columbia, shoots for *New Moon* and *Eclipse*. "*New Moon* wasn't too crazy, and what we discovered was that a large chunk of the American fans—all these young girls—couldn't get into the country, because they didn't have passports. So during the time of *New Moon* and right after, all the fans got their passports. By the time of *Eclipse*, they were there in droves."

By the time of *Breaking Dawn*, shot partly in Louisiana, not only were there dedicated media outlets angling for coverage, but fan-generated websites kept track of actor sightings at local eateries. "Sometimes we'd arrive at locations, and fans would be there before we were," says Bill. "That was a surprise."

Typically the early posting of fan-captured or paparazzi photos from an on-location shoot caused much hand-wringing for the filmmakers. And true to form, within hours of *Breaking Dawn* starting its one-hundred-day shoot on a public but closed-off street in Brazil, pictures of Robert Pattinson and Kristen Stewart were up on the Web. Back in Los Angeles, production executive Gillian Bohrer was on a fan site and noticed them immediately. But her first thoughts were, *Why is Robert's hair so dark?* and *Why aren't he and Kristen wearing wedding rings if this is a honeymoon scene?* She called producer Wyck Godfrey, who was on set, and after getting over the initial shock that he was getting instantaneous studio notes from thousands of miles away, the production was able to make the necessary changes sooner instead of later.

"It was pretty funny," recalls Gillian. "Normally it would have been at least two days before I'd seen any footage. Every now and then, the paparazzi do come in handy." ■

Mackenzie Foy as
RENESMEE CULLEN

In BREAKING DAWN, the introduction of Renesmee as Bella and Edward's offspring poses a lot of questions to the vampire world: Is she a dreaded immortal child? Or a creature not worth fearing? The character had the filmmakers asking a big question, too: How do you visualize a child who rapidly goes from baby size to seven years old in one unified portrayal?

The answer lay in a cutting-edge combination of human performance and computer wizardry. Using a technique made famous by *The Curious Case of Benjamin Button*—in which Brad Pitt's face is seen on the body of a shrunken old man—the masterminds at effects company Lola would digitally graft a single actress's face onto female children of various ages, from infancy on up. *Breaking Dawn - Part 2* visual effects supervisor Terry Windell explains, "It was important that this truly looked like that child, like the person cast as the final Renesmee, and that it not be a series of look-alike actors."

The chosen Renesmee was actress Mackenzie Foy, who floored *Breaking Dawn* director Bill Condon when he first saw her on tape. "I thought, if Rob and Kristen had a baby and she was eight years old, this is what she'd be like. It was incredible!" ▸

Concept art for Renesmee for *Breaking Dawn - Part 2*

BELLA (V.O.)
"There is sweet music here..."

INT. BELLA & EDWARD'S COTTAGE - NURSERY - NIGHT

Bella lies next to Renesmee, (now the size of a 6 yr old) reading Tennyson to her...

BELLA
... "That softer falls than petals from blown roses on the grass, or night dews on still waters..."

She sees Renesmee's eyes shutting.

BELLA
"...Music that brings sweet sleep down from the blissful skies...."

Bella closes the book. She reaches for the light when --

RENESMEE
Mom...
(off Bella's look)
Did Aunt Alice and Uncle Jasper run away because we're going to die?

Bella is surprised. Sees the fear in Renesmee's eyes. She pulls her close.

BELLA
No, Renesmee...
(then)
I think they left to make us safer. That's why all these people are here, too.

Bella kisses her forehead, pulls her even closer.

BELLA
I won't let anyone hurt you. Ever.

Off Bella, mind working, determined to keep this promise...

🎞 DIRECTOR'S TAKE

Watching Kristen Stewart and Mackenzie Foy together on set was special, says *Breaking Dawn* director Bill Condon. Considering Kristen's origins in the business, once having played daughter to another former child star, Academy Award–winner Jodie Foster, in *Panic Room*, Bill could see something being passed down through the generations.

"Kristen's not a mother yet, but she has a huge maternal side," says Bill. "There was something about having a child actor there for Kristen, where she became very protective of Mackenzie in terms of the whole experience. And I think that became the way she found that maternal feeling, even if they were only eleven or twelve years apart."

➤ Mackenzie's work was anything but simple: On set, besides her performance as Renesmee for all scenes in which the character is her own size, she also closely observed filming of the body doubles used to represent Renesmee at younger ages. These child stand-ins had tracking dots on their faces to capture every movement for the effects artists. Months later, in postproduction, Mackenzie was refilmed with what Terry calls "witness cameras"—high-resolution digital cameras—that recorded her matching the head movements of the stand-ins, so they could be meticulously patched in.

Mackenzie proved herself to be a pro. "She's incredibly technically adept," Bill says, adding with a laugh, "She gets this process better than I do."

Michael Sheen echoes the sentiment. "She's such a lovely person, but also a fantastic actress," says the actor, who has a key moment with her in *Part 2*. "It's probably my favorite moment of all the films, when Aro meets Renesmee. Mackenzie knew that was my favorite bit, and she did a drawing of it for me. It's on my fridge as I speak."

"She does a lot of drawing," adds Nikki Reed, who spent a lot of time with Mackenzie and her mother during filming. "She makes pictures for people. She's really awesome, really smart and adultlike. For being such an intelligent, aware little girl, she was sort of unaffected by the set she was on, and I think that's because she has an awesome mom." ■

Renesmee concept art

133

WHO'S WHO:
THE VAMPIRES OF *PART 2*

IRISH COVEN

MARLANE BARNES as Maggie
"Maggie's power is that she knows whether or not people are lying. So when Aro is assessing the child, his words are kind, but my character is suspicious."

AMAZON COVEN

JUDI SHEKONI as Zafrina
"Zafrina can make anyone see anything she wants them to see. That could be fun, although I could probably get into a lot of trouble with that one."

TRACEY HEGGINS as Senna
"My outfit's a whole lot of sexy. I had all these little shells. They called me Bells 'cause on set you could hear me coming a mile away!"

EGYPTIAN COVEN

OMAR METWALLY as Amun
"Amun is the leader of the Egyptian coven. I saw him as a very pragmatic thinker and a survivor. Of course, when I learned I was going to be playing a vampire, I'd be lying if I said that the twelve-year-old in me wasn't jumping up and down."

ANDREA GABRIEL as Kebi
"Most vampires had to wear tiny belts and high heels, but I'm wearing sandals and a long, flowy, elegant dress covered by a scarf. I didn't have to worry about munching all day on set and then my belt being too tight—I lucked out!"

ANGELA SARAFYAN as Tia
"Tia's a strong, independent woman, more of a rocker, and very different from Kebi, who's an older vampire. So when Benjamin and Tia see an opportunity to stand up for something, to fight against authority, they move forward."

RAMI MALEK as Benjamin
"Benjamin is an Egyptian who wants change, who wants freedom, so it's a good story for kids to watch and see a young character out there willing to fight for a greater good."

DENALI COVEN

CHRISTIAN CAMARGO as Eleazar
"Eleazar is Spanish in inception. Well, Spanish via Alaska with beautiful blond Eastern bloc siblings. The Denalis are the best-dressed group. Some people will deny that, but it's true."

MIA MAESTRO as Carmen
"Carmen has a little bit of a rock-and-roll thing to her. She wears leather pants and high boots, and fake fur, which I guess is because we pretend that we feel the cold, coming from the north."

MAGGIE GRACE as Irina
"She's kind of the fulcrum of the story, and to me a very sympathetic and misunderstood character, especially with her family history. Irina is a villain, but hers is a pretty sad story."

MYANNA BURING as Tanya
"If you're a creature that's been around for so very long, and you've chosen to work on your positive qualities, then I think that gives you a certain kind of grace within that's really admirable. That's what I take away from Tanya."

LISA HOWARD as Siobhan
"She was a strong but humble person when she was a human. We're not vegetarians like the Cullens, but I think we're civilized and kind. What you would think Irish peasants would be: stoic, solid, well-meaning people."

PATRICK BRENNAN as Liam
"I'm Irish myself, and I love their toughness, that they're in a lot of pain, and that they fight, drink, and laugh a lot. An Irish vampire is always game for a fight and loyal. And that's Liam, for sure."

AMERICAN NOMADS

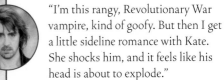

LEE PACE as Garrett
"I'm this rangy, Revolutionary War vampire, kind of goofy. But then I get a little sideline romance with Kate. She shocks him, and it feels like his head is about to explode."

TONI TRUCKS as Mary
"Mary is a true-blue nomad. She doesn't care about having mates. She sticks to her word, and she's very powerful, but that's it. Mary has zero sentimentality and couldn't care less about standing with her coven."

ERIK ODOM as Peter
"This is a guy who lives off the land, who doesn't have a home, isn't used to four walls and a ceiling. Peter's also something of a brawler, more of a roughneck."

VALORIE CURRY as Charlotte
"I remember reading in a book about young Civil War women who would cut off their hair, wear pants, knew how to shoot, to protect themselves. That made me want to do that with Charlotte, because that's where she came from."

BILL TANGRADI as Randall
"According to Stephenie, I was a World War II baby, a baby-boomer vampire, so I'm fairly young in my vampiring years. The way I played it was, if there's a fight, we're here, and if not, we'll go terrorize people elsewhere. Very utilitarian."

ROMANIAN COVEN

GURI WEINBERG as Stefan
"The Romanians were once the rulers of the vampire world and still see themselves that way. But when they have to fight, there's nothing royal about it. It's all animal. Because when they were human and fought, it was vicious. They enjoyed it."

NOEL FISHER as Vladimir
"Vladimir is among the last of a coven that was exterminated, so there's a lot of hate there. They've had thousands of years to seek revenge on the Volturi. That amount of emotional history was fun to bring to the screen."

CASEY LABOW as Kate
"The Denalis are quite stylish, I must say. Lots of furs and leathers. Fortunately, costume designer Michael Wilkinson and I had a similar vision, so I got to pick things that I liked, more or less."

EUROPEAN NOMAD

JOE ANDERSON as Alistair
"Being an outsider who's called in, [I felt] there was a kind of freedom to not conform, really. To be aloof and slightly anarchic. And ultimately there's a great wisdom to him. So I enjoyed Alistair a great deal."

VAMP CAMP

When *The Twilight Saga: Breaking Dawn* shoot turned its attention to the showdown with the Volturi in *Part 2*, a massive indoor equestrian center in Baton Rouge, Louisiana, was turned into a Vampire's Last Stand of sorts. It took weeks to put this climactic sequence on film, and for all the new cast members playing the assembled covens and nomads, there was a lot of downtime to make friends, make merry—and even make director Bill Condon dance.

ERIK ODOM (Peter): A lot of us were in this hotel together, the Hilton, so we had a lot of time to bond. People have termed it Vamp Camp, a bunch of us running around without too many responsibilities, just making sure we were ready for our shoot date.

TONI TRUCKS (Mary): We would just migrate down to the hotel restaurant and bar area in the evenings, or walk around the lobby in our socks.

TRACEY HEGGINS (Senna): It was almost like *Cheers*, because there was always somebody downstairs if you were feeling lonely.

EXT. CULLEN HOUSE - BACKYARD (CONTINUOUS) - DAY

Eleazar continues his approach, joining them. Carlisle is with him. Kate and Garrett join as well. In the background, Alistair lounges on the lawn watching with an enigmatic expression. Edward looks at Eleazar, surprised --

                    EDWARD
          A shield?

                    ZAFRINA
          Lucky for her, since she fights like a child.

Bella turns to Edward --

                    BELLA
          What's a shield?

                    EDWARD
          The ones I've met are so different --

Kate suddenly grabs Bella's arm --

BELLA'S POV - again, a slight GLIMMER where Kate touches her. Otherwise, nothing happens.

                    KATE
          She's a shield all right. That should have put
          her on her ass.

                    GARRETT
          Or your voltage has been exaggerated.

                    KATE
          Maybe it only works on the weak.

She extends her palm. It's a challenge. Garrett grins --

                    CARLISLE
          Garrett, I wouldn't --

-- Garrett touches Kate with his finger. ZAP! His knees buckle and he hits the ground with a hard THUD. Kate stands over him. A smile lights up his face.

                    GARRETT
          You. Are an amazing woman.

ANDREA GABRIEL (Kebi): There was a lot of intermingling of covens. In a good way! Not in a lurid way! And the hotel was so nice, putting up with us. I would come down to the concierge and say, "Have you had enough of needy actors? And can I ask for one more thing?"

BILL TANGRADI (Randall): I remember the first night, Omar Metwally, Casey LaBow, and I saddled up at a local drinking spot and got to know each other. I was a bit of a ringleader socially, rallying the troops to go to a few places in downtown Baton Rouge.

RAMI MALEK (Benjamin): Billy will do anything for you. We were all trying to get other jobs while we were on this movie because there was so much downtime, so he was putting people on tape left and right, sending stuff to New York or L.A., wherever anyone needed. ➤

(OPPOSITE PAGE, CLOCKWISE FROM TOP LEFT) Judi Shekoni, Tracey Heggins, Marlane Barnes, Lisa Howard, and Patrick Brennan in a campfire scene from *Breaking Dawn - Part 2*. (LEFT) Erik Odom as Peter, followed by Valorie Curry as Charlotte, in *Breaking Dawn - Part 2*.

➤ **VALORIE CURRY (Charlotte):** I was one of the homebodies. I'm not much of a partier. Toni Trucks and I would trade DVDs a lot, order ice cream, and watch movies. I just loved it. I have some great friends from that experience, because we bonded over our shared . . . what's the word . . . *captivity?*

CASEY LABOW (Kate): The Hilton was less Vamp Camp than the trailers at the set, which looked like a traveling circus. You'd see signs like "Volturi Lane." Everybody got into it. There were these little nooks and crannies of people hanging out, because you're often there for hours on end not shooting. So you'd walk past Jamie Campbell Bower's trailer and he'd be blasting music with people. Walk up a little more and there's Jackson Rathbone strolling around playing his banjo-lele. Mia Maestro is in her trailer playing her music and honing the record she's made. It became very boarding school.

MYANNA BURING (Tanya): We also got hit by rain. The ground around our trailers flooded, so they created these interlinking pathways with slabs of wood. And that gave it even more of a music-festival feel.

CHRISTIAN CAMARGO (Eleazar): It was a very long two and a half or three weeks of greenscreen work, shooting the fight sequence. When you're standing on set for that long, you end up relying on your coven to entertain you. So we came up with a lot of on-set jokes and pranks. We came up with our own special powers. Someone teased me that I had the power of boring anyone to death with Shakespeare.

MARLANE BARNES (Maggie): The snow was fake, made of paper, and we had snow fights, much to the chagrin of the costume department. I mean, the only colors we saw were green and white. It definitely got a little delirious. There was a lot of musical-theater singing, too. A lot of *West Side Story*, because we were in groups like the Sharks and the Jets. Inevitably somebody would start snapping their fingers.

TRACEY: The Romanians—Guri and Noel—stood behind us, and we would give them Madonna songs to sing in a Romanian accent. It was beyond hilarious. Noel rapped in his accent.

NOEL FISHER (Vladimir): Toni Trucks came up with this great game called Poop Movies. You take any movie title, and it just becomes infinitely more funny if you imagine the movie is about poop. Hilarious, but ridiculously immature.

GURI WEINBERG (Stefan): There were a lot of dumb games. One started by Christian Camargo and Lee Pace involved kicking each other in the shins. One time I kicked Christian and Mia Maestro was there, so she comes over and says, "Why did you do that?" I said, "It's a game." She said, "What is wrong with you guys?"

LEE PACE (Garrett): I like to do jokes on set. Usually Christian Camargo is my target, but we were on that set for such a long time, I thought, *We need to do something to spice this up.* On karaoke night in town, Mia and MyAnna would sing the Eurythmics' "Sweet Dreams," and that's when we came up with the flash mob. Mia and MyAnna really put it together.

MIA MAESTRO (Carmen): It was going to be a dance-off between the Cullens and the Volturi. I decided to put together this choreography for all the Cullen vampires, so that when Bill Condon said "Action!" we would just start dancing to the sound of the Eurythmics. MyAnna and I put a couple of steps together when we were doing hair and makeup. Then we called Toni, because Toni's a really great dancer.

TONI: Mia and MyAnna didn't know how to teach it, and I come from a musical-theater background, so I got the counts, and we got everybody to come on their lunch break, and we taught this dance to the entire cast. We rehearsed, and we told the cinematographer that we would be doing it. But Bill didn't know.

MIA: I was running around getting permission, talking to the sound people, saying, "Okay, I burned the track for you. When I do this sign . . ." It was very James Bond. Nobody knew except one of the producers. But the Volturi were like, "We don't want to do it." I said, "You have to dance back!"

TONI: The time came, and Bill called "Action!" and then Peter Facinelli steps forward and yells over to Michael Sheen, "I think we should settle this battle with a dance-off!" Then all of a sudden we all run to the middle, I'm at the head, and we do this whole dance. It was hysterical. And Bill starts crying from laughing!

The Cullens and their vampire allies have a campfire chat before the Volturi showdown in *Breaking Dawn - Part 2.*

TRACEY: I thought it was pretty awesome. We wanted a real hard dance battle, but the Volturi weren't ready for it.

LEE: The original idea was that we would start coming up, and the Volturi would come up. I just don't think they were interested. Joke's on them—we outdanced them!

CHARLIE BEWLEY (Demetri): We were the Volturi. We don't dance.

MICHAEL SHEEN (Aro): Volturi never have to prepare anything. They just *have* the moves. Thousands of years of moves to draw on. Actually, it was wonderful. And it felt quite naughty, because we were about to go for a take, and then this music started playing. Having worked on the one set every day for weeks and weeks of everyone standing around, it was such a release of joy. Everyone just laughed so much.

MIA: We danced for fifteen minutes straight; everyone, all the actors on set. We destroyed the fake snow.

TONI: Everyone has to wear these little booties to walk on the snow, so they don't get it dirty. Well, Bill is so excited, he takes off his booties and starts circling them in the air. It was amazing. So fun.

BILL CONDON (Director, *Breaking Dawn*): It was thrilling. I was so moved by it. The idea that they were able to keep it a secret was unbelievable, and that they were all good! It was a very generous thing. Talk about practical jokes that lift a mood. I'll never forget that. ▪

Melissa describes the next twenty seconds as an internal dramatic epic of heart-pounding scenarios and excuses coursing through her brain: *I'd put the DVD on top of the car.... Can I pretend they didn't give it to me?... It could have fallen anywhere along the way home.... That's a thirty-minute drive.... Oh God, if it landed in the wrong hands, it would go straight on the Internet....*

Melissa realized that if the worst possible version of *Eclipse*—raw footage, undecided takes, without visual effects, not color-timed—made its way onto the Web, it might mean nobody goes to see it when it eventually gets released. "I'm breaking out in a sweat realizing I may have just cost the studio hundreds of millions of dollars," recalls Melissa. "By the time I get inside, I'm crying, and my husband is like, 'What's going on?'"

As she relayed her tale of woe through a wall of tears, Melissa's husband (a director himself who's worked in film and television) sprang into action. First, he had Melissa call the postproduction house to get them to look for the DVD.

"So I called, I told my husband, and he said, 'Did you speak to the head of post?' I said, 'No, I spoke with the assistant.' He said, 'Call them back. Get the HEAD OF POST.' I did, and she mobilized all twenty people in that editing room to look in the parking lot."

The call came back: It wasn't in the parking lot.

Which meant it was on the street. Anywhere between there and home. A half-hour drive. Miles and miles and miles of Los Angeles roadway, filled with people who could have picked up the DVD and grasped its value.

It's probably hard not to start thinking about ramifications at that point, and Melissa did. "I will single-handedly have destroyed an entire franchise," she says, describing what was going through her head. "That will be my legacy. That's who I'll be. In my old age, I will be that person." ➤

LOSING IT

With her screen adaptations of the TWILIGHT books, and their combined worldwide gross likely to cross the $3 billion mark with *Breaking Dawn - Part 2*, Melissa Rosenberg was recently crowned by the *Hollywood Reporter* as the highest-grossing female screenwriter in Hollywood. "Just to be one of the only women to ever write an entire franchise gives me personal pride," says Melissa. "You feel like you've made your mark a little bit."

It only seems appropriate, then, that in the wake of such success, Melissa should reveal for the first time anywhere what she considers, in her words, "the *worst* moment of my career." And—*gulp*—it also involved the series. It happened during the early stages of editing *Eclipse*—during the winter of 2010—when Melissa was asked to watch a rough early cut of the movie at the postproduction house in Hollywood where director David Slade was assembling it. Because the possibility existed that voice-over would be needed, she was there all day tossing ideas around with David and the producers. Eventually, it was determined that Melissa should take a DVD copy of the movie home so she could work on it.

"I've been in this dark room the entire day, the blood sugar is low, I've been completely caffeinated the whole day, I walk out with my cup of coffee and the DVD, get in the car, and drive home," says Melissa, recalling how it was only when she pulled into her driveway and leaned over to collect her belongings that she realized "the DVD's not there." ➤

> Her focused husband wouldn't allow her to wallow, though, and insisted they get in the car and head back to the location of the postproduction facilities. Halfway there, Melissa got a call. They found . . . the jewel case. No DVD. Truly the worst news. With the seriousness of the situation increasing, it was time to figure out how to tell the people at Summit Entertainment. Time to start thinking damage control. An e-mail to draft. Even if it was to be recovered, Melissa realized, the studio will now know what she did: "I'd be the person who can't be trusted with a DVD."

Five minutes later, another call. This time, the best news: The DVD was found. A production assistant located it in the bushes at Santa Monica Boulevard and Formosa, not far from the post house. So while *anyone* could have happened upon it, luckily the right person did.

And because it was found before SEND had been hit on that dreaded e-mail, the studio never knew. "Until now," notes Melissa, who has come to terms with telling the world of her worst day as a professional writer. "Hey, I'm done with the movies. They can't fire me!" ∎

JUDI SHEKONI
LOOKS BACK

For new cast members joining the *Twilight* franchise at the end, the security measures made clear to everyone—don't tell anyone you've been cast until we say it's okay, don't give away details, no picture-taking on set—were daunting, as Judi Shekoni recalls. Cast as Amazonian coven member Zafrina for *The Twilight Saga: Breaking Dawn - Part 2*, Judi says, "You didn't know what you could and couldn't talk about."

Paranoia about her script falling into the wrong hands, for instance, led her mind to spiral in sweat-inducing directions. "You were really concerned something might happen. I remember my script was in my car a few times, and I was like, 'What if my car gets stolen, and I lose the script?!?' Yeah, if my car had been stolen, I would have been more concerned that the script would go than my car! So yeah, everything went completely out of proportion."

NOT ONLY VAMPIRES LIVE ON...

With the release of *The Twilight Saga: Breaking Dawn - Part 2*, a five-year cinematic journey of hard work, beautiful vampires, and artfully rendered romance will come to an end for those involved in putting together the movie versions of Stephenie Meyer's adored quartet. For fans, one chapter in their devotion to the saga—built around posters, trailers, premieres, trips to multiplexes, and viewing parties at home—will have ended. But, as with all enduring parts of the culture, *Twilight* will live on.

For one thing, the movies have only enhanced the stature of the novels. "The books were always a big seller to start with," notes Laura Byrne-Cristiano of the fan site Twilight Lexicon. "Stephenie had thousands of people at book signings for BREAKING DAWN before there was even a movie out. But I think the movies brought the books from what I would call superstar level to stratosphere level. I know so many people who saw the movie and then picked up all the books."

Summit Entertainment co-chair Rob Friedman says the *Twilight* franchise was instrumental in establishing young adult books as a viable genre for adapting to film. "I think a whole new cultural phenomenon in young adult entertainment has been introduced," he says. "*Twilight* will forever be remembered as setting a stage that will continue in film. Young adult literature is a very big focus of Hollywood now."

Since the story is built on the desire of a young woman, whose romantic quest spurred females of all ages around the world to follow along, Summit Entertainment president of worldwide marketing Nancy Kirkpatrick sees the *Twilight* legacy in gender terms. "One of its strongest cultural impacts has to do with the power of women," says Nancy. "Once entertainment companies grasp how much buying power and clout young women possess, then they'll realize all their energies don't have to go toward stories of men with weapons fighting aliens. It's especially wonderful, I think, that this was a series about eternal love." *New Moon* director Chris Weitz even sees life for *The Twilight Saga* in the halls of academia. "I'm sure it will be the subject of PhDs in about ten years," Chris says.

Kristen Stewart is aware of how rare it is to see a female-driven franchise. "It's what I want to keep doing," she says. "Not exclusively, obviously. But it's definitely something to note. It's pretty remarkable, and pretty cool."

Of course, the *Twilight* movies turned Kristen, Robert Pattinson, and Taylor Lautner into superstars—household names who now have a hard time buying milk at the corner store unnoticed. But unlike the manufactured stars of other movies, the outpouring of interest from fans was there before the first movie came out because of their love for the characters, and this devotion was fortified by the rewarding performances they got in return. It led to a relationship between talent and fan that's been unique in modern movies. "The fans are the people we make these movies for," says Taylor. "We wanted to bring these characters to life for fans who have known them longer than we have. They know these characters inside and out. And though as an actor you want to bring parts of yourself to a role, you had to be careful because you're playing a character that millions of fans are in love with. It was extra pressure on us." ➤

Known for their deep devotion to Stephenie Meyer's stories, Twilight fans have helped make the movies an international phenomenon, and turned Robert Pattinson, Kristen Stewart, and Taylor Lautner into megastars.

> And that passion was ultimately rewarding in and of itself, says Michael Sheen. "The enthusiasm and excitement people have for these stories and for the characters, and the world of it, was really wonderful," he explains. "Just to see that that can still happen. So to be a part of that has been great."

For its myriad young stars, some just starting their careers, revisiting a role every year turned into a form of school, a *Twilight* college of sorts, creating learning experiences, good times, strange times, and lasting friendships. We watched quite a few people grow up over five movies. "It's like [the actors] were in this bubble," says Julia Jones. "This translucent bubble, and you can't really leave it, but everybody can sort of see in." That shared feeling generated a sense of loyalty, she adds, "particularly in the beginning, when things were starting to get crazy."

But craziness can be channeled wisely, as cast member Michael Welch found out when he got involved with an organization doing good works in distressed countries. As Michael explains, "The Twilight community did a campaign, and purely from fans we were able to raise enough money to build a clean-water well in the African country Swaziland and do a rehabilitation project in Uganda. Between those two projects, it's going to provide clean water to about a thousand people in the short term and generations in the long term. Here, Stephenie creates this world purely out of her imagination, and somehow that's connected to a thousand people having clean water who otherwise wouldn't have had it. It's remarkable to me. To be a part of that is just a gift. It's awesome!"

In the years since Stephenie turned her legendary dream into an addictive series of novels, and those books were turned into a globally successful movie franchise, Twilight has been a shining example of the power of the love story—the thrill when love is new and different, the sadness when it feels unattainable, the confusion when it's threatened, and the joy when it's celebrated.

When producer Wyck Godfrey reflects on the saga, those sentiments come to mind. "As a parent, it's a comforting message of love being deep, romantic, and emotional; that it's about 'Who is the perfect person for me?' Where love is something in which you'd do anything for that person to protect them. And that you can love in different ways. There's the best friend you love, and the stop-your-heart person you love. And that there's room in your life for both. That's a great message." ∎

THE TWILIGHT SAGA TIMELINE

APR. 2004

Paramount Pictures takes out an option on Stephenie Meyer's soon-to-be-published novel, TWILIGHT.

FEB. 2008
Taylor Lautner is cast as Jacob Black.

APR. 2007
Summit Entertainment obtains the rights to TWILIGHT, and the movie enters preproduction.

AUG. 7, 2007
ECLIPSE is published.

DEC. 2007
Robert Pattinson is cast as Edward Cullen.

NOV. 2007
Kristen Stewart is cast as Bella Swan.

NOV. 17, 2008
Twilight premieres in Los A at the Mann Village Theat

Principal photography on the *Twilight* movie is completed.

More than 6,500 Twilight fans flock to the San Diego Comic-Con.

The book series concludes with the final installment, BREAKING DAWN.

MAY 8, 2008

JUL. 24, 2008

AUG. 2, 2008

NOV. 4, 2008
Twilight sound track debuts at #1 on the Billboard 200. Selling more than 3.5 million copies worldwide, it becomes the most successful movie sound track since *Chicago*.

NOV. 10, 2008
A twelve-city mall tour kicks off at San Francisco's Stonestown Galleria. When thousands of fans hoping to see Robert Pattinson line up earlier than expected, havoc ensues.

NOV. 21, 2008
Twilight opens in theaters and on the first night grosses $7 million from midnight showings before making $35.7 million in total throughout its first day.

NOV. 20, 2009
New Moon opens with the biggest midnight showing in U.S. history, earning an estimated $26.3 million.

NOV. 16, 2009
New Moon premieres in Los Angele at the Mann Village Theatre. Fans started camping out four days prior

APR. 23, 2010
The trailer for *Eclipse* debuts on *The Oprah Winfrey Show*.

JUN. 17, 2010
A full week before the scheduled premiere for *Eclipse* at the 7,000-seat Nokia Theatre, fans begin forming a tent city at Nokia Plaza.

FEB. 11, 2010
It's announced that *Breaking Dawn* will be split into two separate movies.

JUN. 8, 2010
Eclipse sound track is released.

JUN. 24, 2010
Eclipse premieres in Los Angeles.

JUN. 30, 2010
Eclipse opens and shatters box-office record taking $30.1 million at midnight screenings in the U.S. and going on to net $68.5 million its first day.

NOV. 16, 2012
Breaking Dawn - Part 2 is released, thereby concluding the film saga.

APR. 16, 2012
A year after filming officially wrapped, director Bill Condon reveals that the cast will reunite to film some additional shots for *Breaking Dawn - Part 2*.

OCT. 5, 2005

TWILIGHT is published and becomes an instant bestseller.

NEW MOON hits shelves.

SEPT. 6, 2006

NOV. 23, 2008

Over its first weekend, *Twilight* goes on to gross $69.6 million in the U.S., becoming the biggest opening weekend ever for a film helmed by a female director.

MAR. 21, 2009

Twilight is released on DVD and sells more than 3 million copies on its first day.

MAR. 23, 2009

New Moon is scheduled to begin shooting in Vancouver on this day, but cameras actually start rolling a few days early.

MAR. 9, 2009

Dakota Fanning officially joins the cast of *New Moon* as Jane.

MAY 31, 2009

Twilight wins Best Movie at the MTV Movie Awards as well as Breakthrough Performance for Robert Pattinson and Best Female Performance for Kristen Stewart.

JUN. 9, 2009

The trailer for *New Moon* breaks online records with 4.5 million views worldwide in twenty-four hours.

JAN. 7, 2009

After fan speculation to the contrary, Stephenie Meyer announces on her website that Taylor Lautner will return as Jacob Black in the film of NEW MOON.

AUG. 17, 2009

Eclipse begins shooting at Vancouver Film Studios.

JUL. 28, 2009

It is announced that Bryce Dallas Howard will replace Rachelle Lefevre as Victoria in the film adaptation of ECLIPSE.

OCT. 16, 2009

Sound track to *New Moon* is released. When it reaches #1 on the Billboard 200 a week later, it's the first time both a sound track and its sequel have ever had that distinction.

AUG. 9, 2009

Twilight sweeps the board at the Teen Choice Awards, taking ten awards, including the Choice Movie Liplock for Robert Pattinson and Kristen Stewart.

NOV. 1, 2010

Filming begins on *Breaking Dawn - Part 1* and *Part 2*.

NOV. 18, 2011

Breaking Dawn - Part 1 is released and takes in $705 million worldwide, hitting the $500 million mark in record time at the box office.

NOV. 8, 2011

The sound track for *Breaking Dawn - Part 1* is released.

NOV. 14, 2011

Breaking Dawn - Part 1 premieres in Los Angeles at the Nokia Theatre.

APR. 22, 2011

Kristen Stewart and Robert Pattinson film their final scenes together on Saint Thomas in the Caribbean.

SUMMIT ENTERTAINMENT

REQUESTS THE HONOR OF YOUR PRESENCE

AT THE RECEPTION FOR THE PREMIERE OF

THE TWILIGHT SAGA: BREAKING DAWN – PART 1

MONDAY, THE FOURTEENTH OF NOVEMBER

TWO THOUSAND AND ELEVEN

TEN O'CLOCK IN THE EVENING

LA LIVE EVENT DECK

LOS ANGELES

SCREENING TICKET
ADMIT ONE
Strictly Nontransferable

SCREENING TICKET
ADMIT ONE
Strictly Nontransferable

MANN VILLAGE THEATRE
961 BROXTON AVENUE
WESTWOOD

SECTION _____ ROW _____ SEAT _____

the twilight saga

new moon

SUMMIT ENTERTAINME
INVITES YOU AND A GUE

THE NEW MOON PA

IMMEDIATELY FOLLOWING THE SC

HAMMER MUSE
10899 WILSHIRE BOUL
WESTWOOD

PHOTO IDENTIFICATION REQUI

the twilight sag

new mo

PUBLICIS

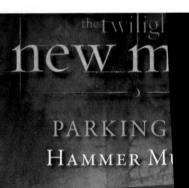

the twilight

new m

PARKING
HAMMER MU

7:30 PM

MANN VILLAGE THEATRE
961 BROXTON AVENUE
WESTWOOD

ACKNOWLEDGMENTS

If anything, a project like this makes it diamond-sparkling clear just how much work goes into putting movies together and sending them out into the world. So, to all the talented individuals who shared their stories, reflections, and insights about the *Twilight* films with me, the heartiest of thank-yous, especially to the time-giving generosity of Melissa Rosenberg, Bill Condon, Catherine Hardwicke, Kristen Stewart, Wyck Godfrey, and their respective teams (like Team Jack). But it all started with the indefatigable and wonderful Eric Kops at Summit Entertainment, whose tireless work in helping me corral interviews can't be overstated, as well as that of his colleagues Mike Rau, Jennifer Curran, Jennifer Smuckler, and Ramzy Zeidan. Special thanks to Summit executive Gillian Bohrer, whose institutional *Twilight* knowledge is a pleasure to behold. Thanks to Little, Brown for the wonderful opportunity, and naturally to Stephenie Meyer for creating characters and a world worth visualizing, cherishing, and writing about in the first place! Then there's Insight Editions, which must have a "hire only nice people" policy: immense thank-yous to my patient, hardworking, and gifted editor Roxanna Aliaga; publisher Raoul Goff; project manager Michael Madden; editor Amy Wideman; and the talented Insight design department, especially Jon Glick. Thank you to my agent, Trena Keating, whose support and advice is invaluable. Also to Denise, fervent Team Abele member and my favorite Twilight fan. And on a personal note, nothing can touch the gratitude and love I have for Margy Rochlin, who makes writing about our generation's biggest love story that much sweeter, since I live one myself. —Robert Abele

ABOUT THE AUTHOR

Award-winning writer and critic Robert Abele covers film and television for many newspapers and magazines. His work has appeared in the *Los Angeles Times*, *Variety*, *Premiere*, *DGA Quarterly*, *Emmy* magazine, and the *New York Post*. He has written a biography of Harrison Ford, co-authored *The Paramount Story*, and collaborated on the *New York Times* bestseller *Official Book Club Selection: A Memoir According to Kathy Griffin*. He lives in Los Angeles, California, with his wife, journalist Margy Rochlin.

Little, Brown and Company

Hachette Book Group
237 Park Avenue, New York, NY 10017
Visit our website at www.lb-teens.com

Little, Brown and Company is a division of Hachette Book Group, Inc.
The Little, Brown name and logo are trademarks of
Hachette Book Group, Inc.

All photos are courtesy of Summit Entertainment.
Extra-special thank-yous to the Summit team: Nancy Kirkpatrick, Jennifer
Smuckler, Andrew Hreha, Amanda Boury, Jill Jones, Asmeeta Narayan, and
Sabryna Phillips. Also Russell Binder of Striker Entertainment for putting
everyone together and making this book possible.

Additional images provided courtesy of Artisan's Designs, Paul Austerberry,
Bill Bannerman, David Brisbin, Caitlin Byrnes, Chad Hudson Events, Bill
Condon, Charles Crossin, Catherine Hardwicke, Carolina Herrera, Tish
Monaghan, Richard Sherman, Skylab Architecture, Tippett Studio, Michael
Wilkinson, and Greg Yolen.

The publisher is not responsible for websites (or their content) that are not
owned by the publisher.

INSIGHT EDITIONS

PO Box 3088
San Rafael, CA 94912
www.insighteditions.com

INSIGHT EDITIONS
Publisher: Raoul Goff
Creative Director: Christine Kwasnik
Production Manager: Anna Wan
Project Manager: Michael Madden
Editor: Roxanna Aliaga
Designer: Jon Glick

First Edition: October 2012

Library of Congress Control Number 2012940139

ISBN: 978-0-316-22246-4

Insight Editions, in association with Roots of Peace, will plant two trees
for each tree used in the manufacturing of this book. Roots of Peace is
an internationally renowned humanitarian organization dedicated to
eradicating land mines worldwide and converting war-torn lands into
productive farms and wildlife habitats. Together, we will plant two million
fruit and nut trees in Afghanistan and provide farmers there with the skills
and support necessary for sustainable land use.

10 9 8 7 6 5 4 3 2 1

Manufactured in China by Insight Editions

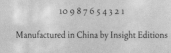